Falling for the Roommate

Clearview Falls University Book #2

S.E. Rose

Sierra Hill

Chapter One

G race

"Hey, toots! Come on down and see what your old man concocted for our last breakfast together!"

I roll over, grabbing my extra pillow to muffle his sing-songy, exuberant voice coming from the kitchen downstairs.

There are times when being the only child of a divorced dad who doesn't have a life of his own is exhausting.

Today is one of those days.

I'm packed and ready to go back to school for the fall semester, but apparently I won't be sleeping in. I was hoping I could have one more lazy morning in my own bedroom before I start my new living arrangement off-campus.

This year is going to be a whole lot different than the first two years at Clearview Falls University. This year, instead of living in the dorms with my two besties, I'm moving into the off-campus house I'll be sharing with my best friend, Lucy, her boyfriend, Emmett, and a bunch of football players.

That includes my new roommate—a rowdy, obnoxious, giant football player whose nickname is *Killer*.

Yes, that's right. They call him Killer. Short for Killian.

Sounds like a very trustworthy roommate to have, doesn't it? He'll probably murder me in my sleep.

I shove the pillow over my face, clutching it tightly with my arms and groan into the soft down. Why the hell did I ever agree to this?

My dad's voice interrupts my thoughts on the ridiculous decision I was forced to make at the end of the last school year when my friend, Kelsie, said she was going to spend the semester abroad in France, and the other, Lucy, will be living in the house with her boyfriend. Which left me solo without a roommate.

"Get down here. You're going to love it, pumpernickel."

That's another thing about my dad. He always calls me by nicknames instead of my actual name. I used to think it was cute, but now as I'm nearing twenty-one, it's kind of annoying.

Don't get me wrong. I love my dad and think he's one of the best guys alive. He's been my one and only constant in the past seven years, along with Lucy. If it hadn't been for them, I'm not sure I'd have survived my parents' divorce after being uprooted from my life in San Fran to live out on a ranch in the middle of the sticks.

But now that I'm ready to begin my junior year, after being at home alone nearly all summer, I need a little space from my dad.

With the exception of a visit back to San Francisco to see my mom—which got cut short due to a business trip to

China she failed to mention to me before I came—I have been stuck on the ranch working with my dad.

I barely even got to see Lucy much because she was working as an assistant at our hometown library or spending time with her Emmett. So it wasn't exactly the summer I'd hoped it would be.

Which is also why I spent hours and hours with my online gaming friends. My games kept me thinking about all the things I've been missing and wanting. It just exacerbated the growing itch in my belly for something more. Something big and extraordinary to happen in my life.

And I'm not just talking about losing my virginity.

Yeah, that's right. I'll be turning twenty-one this fall and I'm still a virgin.

It's the embarrassing secret I've kept hidden from even my closest friends because it makes me feel like a misfit. Like there's something terribly wrong with me.

And maybe there is.

I've never been able to trust a guy enough or wanted to be close enough to go all the way, but that needs to change this year. I have to make it a priority.

The only other priority right now is trying to go back to sleep, but even the pillow can't drown out the noise of the clanking pots and pans from the kitchen of our two-story, custom-built house on the 40-acre property. My dad bought this on a whim when I was thirteen, saying he needed to find his "inner peace and quiet." But at this moment, I don't believe there is any such thing.

Knowing my chill morning has come to an abrupt end, I toss the pillow off my head and reluctantly get out of bed, throwing my hair into a messy bun as I make my way down to the kitchen.

Fred, our orange tabby cat, sits perched on the corner of

the counter, his tail flapping back and forth as he silently observes the mess being made in front of him. Our cattle dog, Barley, waits more or less patiently at dad's side in hopes of catching anything that might get dropped while cooking. Dad is at the stove stirring something that I'll admit smells delicious. Cinnamon and apples.

My dad's latest hobby and obsessions has been watching all the reality cooking shows and then trying to make the recipes even better. Although it creates big messes, and there have been a few misses like the lamb chops he botched, he leans on me to be both his taste tester and his sidekick.

I pad in on bare feet, brushing past Barley and sticking a hand out to pat Fred's head, who looks up at me with curious green eyes, before I turn my attention to my dad.

"Morning," I greet, my voice still froggy from lack of sleep. Although his early morning breakfast has contributed to my sluggishness, it's not the only reason I'm so tired. I may have stayed up a little too late last night playing my favorite internet video game, *Capital Offense*.

It's where I've spent many hours this summer with my online gamer friends who understand me.

Especially one in particular. Someone I've developed a special kind of connection with outside of my dad and my two best friends. I don't know anything about this gamer except what I know through the constant messaging while online. Whether they know it or not, they helped me get through this summer without pulling my hair out or going stir crazy.

My dad swings around with a spatula in his hand, wearing a silly apron and lopsided grin on his face. The sight of him pulls at my heartstrings and already makes me homesick even though I don't leave for school until tomorrow.

"Good morning, graceland." Yet another stupid nickname he often uses for me, but I don't roll my eyes this time. Instead, I rush over and throw my arms around him, crushing my face to the middle of his chest.

"Whoa there, Nelly. I've got a hot cast iron griddle in my hands." He holds out his arms away from me as I reluctantly let go and take a step back. He tips his head, his face covered in a dark scruff, and returns the unspoken sentiment. "I love you, too, toots. And I'm going to miss the heck out of you."

He carries the pan over to the large woodblock island and nods in the direction of the cabinets.

"Why don't you grab us some plates because we need to eat this bad boy while it's still hot."

I reach into the cupboard and take out two plates, setting them down so he can dish them up. I sniff at the aromatic air, scented with the first hints of fall. "It smells delish. What did you make?"

He grins proudly. "It's a Dutch apple pancake. It's from *the Cooking with Cast Iron* show I've been telling you about. Fascinating stuff! I will never go back to using any other cookware."

That's the other truly weird and wonderful thing about my dad. He's a brilliant man who made a fortune in the tech world when he developed, patented and then sold a revolutionary e-commerce software. Yet it's these simple things that give him pleasure in life and make him happy. Although, I'd still like to see him settle down and get married again someday. Or at least date someone.

For now, if he's content with where things are at, so am

I. Which is why I'm following in his footsteps and am majoring in computer science.

The only problem is the closer I get to graduation next year, the more unsettled and restless I feel. I'm not sure if I'm pointed in the right direction for a future career. Like I'm packed and heading off on a beach vacation when I'd really prefer to be in the mountains.

I take my first bite and moan around the fork. "Oh, my God, Dad. This is so good!"

You'd think I'd awarded him the biggest accolade of his career by the expression he gives me. Oh, geez. Are those tears in his eyes too?

He sniffs. "I'm going to miss cooking for you, Gracie girl."

"Dad," I reply softly. "I'm less than an hour away. You know you can stop by at any time with food. I will be living with a houseful of hungry football players."

My dad groans and shakes his head. "Don't remind me. I've blocked out the part where my little girl will be shacking up with a dude named Killer."

He gives me a pointed look. "If he tries to do anything creepy or even looks at you sideways, that's it. You let me know and you're out of there. You hear me?"

I nod reassuringly. "Yeah, Dad. I know. But I promise, Killian isn't like that at all. He may be annoying as hell, like a doofy Golden Retriever puppy, but he's a good guy."

I'm not sure who I'm trying to convince more; my dad or myself.

It's true that Killian Palmer is one of the nicest guys I know. While I'm not exactly tight with him, he's now included in my inner circle and if Emmett trusts him, then so do I.

Unless he gives me cause not to.

* * *

Later, after watching a B-rated movie with my dad, where he, Fred, and Barley, all promptly fell asleep before the ending credits began to play, I head upstairs and log on to see who is playing.

A smile curls up at the corners of my mouth when I see the flashing indicator that my gaming buddy is online and sent me a message sometime this morning.

> BigHardware69: Yo, Ranchhand. You gonna take that shit PosterBoy12 was dishing out last night? Want me to squash him?

I chuckle. I love both the camaraderie and the trash-talking we do in this game. It's a fun way to keep things light with plenty of anonymity. No one even knows I'm a girl. I don't have an avatar with any descriptive features just for that reason.

> RanchHandRAM1: Nah. It's all good. I'm quite capable of fighting my own battles. Just worry about your own stats, bruh. You sucked donkey balls last night.

A new chat box pops up.

> BigHardware69: Ha! My balls are the size of donkey balls, bro. BTW, are you at school yet? Getting any pussy with all that RAM you packing?

I swallow down the heaviness of my lies. Sometimes it can be a bit too much, especially when the topic of sex comes up.

RanchHandRAM1: Dude, you wish you had all this RAM.

BigHardware69: Like I said… the size of DONKEY BALLS!

And with that, I close my laptop and lay down on my bed, a smile still etched on my face as I slowly drift off to LaLaLand.

Chapter Two

K illian

"Give me twenty more," Offensive Coach Lester barks out after the whistle blows.

Emmett and I both groan in a feeble attempt to do twenty more pushups as requested. I hate pushups. I'd literally rather do a thousand crunches or run another two miles than this. But I know the conditioning is an important part of our pre-season training. We need to come back strong this year and hopefully get to the championships and a bowl game in December.

"What's that? Did I hear you guys want to run some drills?" Coach pipes up over all our grumbles and groans.

Sweat pours down the back of my shirt and my forehead, seeping into my eyes. I blink to rid myself of the stinging sensation, but don't stop my movement in fear our coach will think I'm giving him a hard time. The complaints from the team quiet down as the countdown to completion continues on. No one wants to have to run drills or sprints back and forth between the ten and twenty yard lines and then the twenty to thirty yard lines if we can help it. Exhaustion is weighing heavy on us after a summer of less activity.

"At least he's not having us do a pull-up competition like last week," Emmett mumbles between heavy, panting breaths.

I turn my head and glare at him, elbows locking as I push my body upright. "At least you have it easier in that one. Try hefting up this body." I gesture with a nod down my torso.

I'm a big guy, much bigger than my friends. My mom used to say it was all the fresh cow milk I drank growing up on our farm, but I think it might be genetics. My dad and his brother are both enormous too and were both college ballplayers back in the day.

Unlike many of my teammates who lounged around on the beach or lakes this summer, I kept in fairly good shape by working on the farm. When not baling hay, hauling feed, or fixing machinery, I was still focused on strength training.

Earlier this week during our physicals and strength evaluations, my stats proved it. I did the 40-yard in 4.8 seconds, bench pressed 285 pounds, and my squat was a solid 420 pounds. I crushed it and was pretty damn proud of myself.

But at the moment, I feel like I could die.

"Eighteen..." Coach yells out. "Nineteen...Twenty. Okay, boys. Hit the showers."

We all stumble to our feet, grabbing towels and water bottles as they are handed to us and leave the field on the way into the locker room.

I shower up and change into clean clothes, throwing on

some sweatpants and ditching the sweaty garments in the laundry bag at the end of my locker row when Emmett saunters over with a towel wrapped around his waist.

"Lucy mentioned that Grace would be moved in today. Are you ready for your new roommate?" he asks with a wink and a grin.

I shrug noncommittally. I honestly haven't put much thought into it yet except how it might cramp my sex life.

That wasn't something I considered at the end of last spring when I opened my big mouth and invited Lucy's friend, Grace Ford, to become my roommate this year. Had I been thinking about how a girl living in my space might change my lifestyle, I would have just kept quiet instead of jumping in and offering up the other half of my room. The attic floor that I should have had all to myself this year because Tate, the previous occupant, graduated and I was on the list for the space.

But one glance into Grace's dejected face when her friend Kelsie announced she wouldn't be living with her this fall had me extending the outrageous offer. She'd seriously looked so forlorn, as if she'd been orphaned and abandoned by her friends.

Honestly, I was surprised as fuck when, a few days later, she called and accepted my offer.

The thing is, I'm actually a little uncomfortable about it now that the time has come. In theory, living with a girl seems like heaven. However, I've never lived with a girl before. I grew up with two younger brothers at home and have always shared a bedroom and bathroom, so that part won't be new. I've slept with a lot of girls and shared my bed with them, of course. But lived with one? This could prove more difficult than I anticipated.

Grace seems like a cool girl. We hung out a lot at the

end of last year after Emmett started dating Lucy. It was just a natural progression to have Lucy's friends tag along and hang out at our house.

From what I gathered, Grace always seemed a little like the third wheel between Kelsie and Lucy. Lucy was extremely book smart and shy, and Kelsie was as loud and the center of attention as I am in group settings, gaining everyone's attention by her entertaining remarks.

Grace, on the other hand, came across a little more subdued. She seemed like she enjoyed partying and could come out of her shell and have a good time, but was a bit reserved too. Like she could take or leave the crowd and be okay alone and on her own.

From what I know of her, Grace is genuinely good people, so naturally I felt compelled to help her out when the situation arose.

Hopefully the decision doesn't come back to bite me in the ass.

First thing we'll need to do is put some rules in place, just like I did when I roomed with Emmett. If the door is shut and something's on the doorknob, it means go the fuck away!

Emmett begins to change as I stuff my pads and gear in my bag to bring home with me.

"Lucy texted me earlier before practice that she was helping Grace move her boxes of shit upstairs, but she may need our help with some big stuff," Emmett says. "You good with that, Killer?"

"Yeah, sure," I reply, pulling my clean CFU shirt on and slinging my backpack over my shoulder. "I gotta stop by the agricultural center first, but I can help lug stuff upstairs later. I'll catch up with you at the house."

"See you at home," Emmett says as I turn and head out of the building.

I hurry across the field and then the quad toward the ag center, which is on the far end of the campus. CFU is unique in that due to the rural setting, it hosts ample space for the agricultural and equestrian centers. As my major is agricultural business, I spend a huge amount of time at the center. If I'm not out on the football field, in a classroom, or at home, this is where I'm at.

Upon entering the building, I receive a wave of greeting from Professor Schmidt who's in the front office. I stuff my bags in the cubby lockers in the main hallway and head through the adjoining door into the barn to check on Old Bessie, a cow who is due to give birth any day now.

Ah, such a sexy way to spend my afternoon.

Would I rather be hanging out at home with a hot chick in my bedroom right now? Abso-fucking-lutely. But this is what my future entails and I need to be present for this animal husbandry course and do my duties to pass and graduate next year.

"Hey there, sweet girl," I murmur, rubbing along her severely swollen, distended belly as I enter her pen. "Who's ready for mommyhood?"

"She's been restless all morning," Professor Schmidt calls out from the interior office. "But I don't think today is the day."

"That's good. But you'll text me if anything changes, right?" I add some hay to her trough and some more padding on the floor, raking up the pieces strewn around. Just like any animal, a mother-to-be will always nest prior to the arrival of her offspring. It's one of my jobs to keep things neat and tidy.

"You know I will, Killian. But Old Bessie's a pro here.

She's done this a number of times. Now shouldn't you be getting to work on that research project? The time is going to go by fast this semester, especially once football starts." He raises an eyebrow in a mock scolding manner.

Professor Schmidt is my independent research project advisor this term and he's letting me get a head start on it to accommodate my crazy football practice schedule.

I'm still trying to work out exactly what I'm going to be researching and writing about. One topic that's of personal interest to me is the demise of small family farms in the Midwest. It's a topic I know way too much about, given I've seen the feast or famine that comes along with being a farmer. I'm hoping the research I conduct will help me to learn something to help improve the efficiency on my parents' farm.

"Yeah, yeah," I grumble, but I flash him my lopsided grin and leave through the side door of the barn that runs parallel to the street where we live.

By the time I walk back to the house we've occupied since our sophomore year, I'm bone tired and hungrier than a bear. I just want to eat a whole pizza and play video games on the couch, and then crash.

When I arrive, the house is bustling with some of my teammates, a few of their girlfriends, and various other girls I've seen around on campus. That's the perk of being a football player. There is never a shortage of hot women wanting to hang out. I say my "hellos" and climb the two flights of stairs to the attic.

I grin when the "penthouse" sign comes into view. Emmett thought it was fitting and bought it for me for my birthday this summer, ceremoniously hanging it over the door. Two floors below, it's a party, but up here, it's relatively quiet except for the sound of a keyboard clicking. It must be Grace.

Keeping the smile on my face, I open the door to our now shared bedroom...and then freeze. I didn't expect to see this.

"What in the amber waves of grain is going on here?" I ask incredulously, my jaw dropping when I look around the room and take in its appearance, a far cry from the state I left it in this morning.

And now...it's...clean.

And I'm not talking just tidied up. I mean it's *clean*-clean. I'm pretty sure I could eat off my dresser. Wait, I have a dresser? Was that there before?

I move in a semi-circle and take in the appearance of the room and then take a gigantic sniff at the air.

Holy fuck, it smells like a lavender field in here.

I want to take a step back outside and double-check that this is indeed the same room I vacated early this morning when I left for practice. Either that, or I've stepped through some time portal because it looks a hell of a lot different.

I'll admit, I may be a little messy—okay, a slob—but what college dude isn't? But this...shit. This is taking it to a whole new level. Maybe my new roommate has OCD or something?

My eyes track around the room and then land on the one-and-only culprit sitting cross-legged on her bed. A bed adorned and piled high with a flowery comforter, and lots and lots of freaking pink, green, and purple pillows. Jesus Christ. It looks like a Van Gogh exhibit in here.

Grace's head pops up over her laptop screen, her dark brown eyes peering at me proudly, as if she's expecting some sort of congratulatory accommodation.

"Welcome home, roomie. Hope you don't mind, but I

figured while I was moving in, I'd straighten your side up a bit."

My voice is laced with panic, my eyes wide with bewilderment. "What the hell did you do with all my stuff?"

I walk around the far end of the attic, searching as if we were in the midst of playing a game of hot and cold and Grace is going to give me the clues.

"I put it all away. Your clothes are exactly where they should be in the built-in drawers over there and in the closet." She points in the direction of the oversized closet taking up one wall of the attic room. "All your manly toiletries are in the bathroom. Oh, and as a one-time courtesy, I washed your stinky clothes that were on the floor and threw out the half-eaten burrito under your jeans. That was just plain nasty," she states with a sour grimace.

I'm momentarily shell-shocked. Normally I'm considered a pretty even-keeled, affable guy who can go with the flow. But this...this goes above and beyond what a new roommate should do without permission.

"Grace, I was saving that for later! I was going to eat it now," I lie, tossing my bag of stinky practice clothes on the bed. I'm half-minded to open it and dump the contents out on the floor just to spite her.

And fine, I really wasn't saving it. I completely forgot about it during our late night run to the Border when I was pretty drunk and was going to toss it out the next morning. So she did save me the trouble, but I'm not about to admit that. Has she ever heard about asking?

She rolls her eyes and gags. "Your side of the room was a class five disaster area. I was ready to call in FEMA."

"Whatever. It was merely organized chaos. I knew exactly where everything was." Another non-truth because I'm usually running late and in search of clean underwear and T-shirts before 7:00 a.m. practice. I grumble, rummaging around to locate my things, still a little pissed she would take liberties like this without first consulting me.

I mean, it's not like I asked for her to do this. She's not my mother.

"Organized chaos?" she snorts indignantly. "I think we can hold on to the organized part." Her voice is sarcastic, but teasing, and does little to quell my annoyance.

So far, living with a girl sucks balls.

"Where the hell did you put my shoes?" I ask, voice rising to a high-pitched level, kneeling down to search under the bed where normal people keep their sneakers.

"In the closet...on a...wait for it...*shoe rack,*" she says with a wink. Like I'm supposed to be impressed by this update.

"Very funny," I sneer. "I don't have a shoe..." My words trail off when I slide open the closet door to find my shoes neatly stacked on a freaking shoe rack. I let out a loud cough of exasperation. "I stand corrected. What about my hats? I always wear baseball caps."

"You're hot," she says.

I whip my head around to stare at her, wide-eyed. Did she just call me hot? That's random as hell and completely unexpected. But I guess everything I've learned so far about my new roommate has been unexpected.

She lets out a laugh. "Hot or cold? As in, you're hot, you're on fire...getting warmer."

I furrow my brow. Is she a damn mind reader? How did she know I was just thinking of that game? I turn to my left and find my caps all neatly hung on little hooks.

"Ding, ding, ding!" She taps her nose with a finger. "We have a winner, folks!"

I can tell I'm getting hangry as I rip a ball cap down off

the hook and fit it backwards on my head. If I'm going to be able to put up with this total neat freak in my living space—which was totally fine without her meddling cleanliness—then I'm going to need two pepperoni pizzas and probably a gallon of pop STAT.

This situation with the room will have to wait until I'm fully fed and can gather my thoughts on this research project before the season takes over my life, along with my other classes and agricultural center responsibilities.

I open my food delivery app on my phone. "I'm ordering food. Do you want any pizza or pop?"

Laughter fills the room and I steal a glance at her from my phone. "Pop?" she repeats, sarcasm lacing her tone. She lowers the laptop lid so that I can see her whole face. "Did you just call it *pop*?"

"Yes, *pop*," I state, letting the P literally pop from my mouth. Now besides hangry, I'm irritated and confused by this woman. Please don't tell me she's one of those no-sugar-no-sweets healthy lifestyle eaters. That would be just great.

"You know, the sugary delicious drink?"

I'm beginning to question everything about this living arrangement when there's a knock on the open door. I spin around and find Emmett and Lucy standing there looking thrilled to see us.

"Yo, how's it going in here? You getting all settled in, Grace?" Emmett steps in, his eyes grow wide, and he staggers back. "Whoa, is this the same room?"

I glower at Emmett and nudge my chin toward Grace's bed. Lucy circles around him, plopping down to sit next to Grace.

"This is all her doing...I'm just about to order some pizza and pop since it looks like we won't have any heavy lifting to do. You guys want in?"

"Yeah, Grace, do you want any *pop*?" Lucy snickers, nudging her friend in the shoulder.

My lips turn down in a frown as I enter a new stage of confusion. "What in fuck's name is going on? What the hell is wrong with the use of the word pop?"

Lucy giggles and Grace glares at her.

"Grace thinks it's weird to call soda, *pop*. When she first moved from the West Coast, she'd never heard it called that before. And let me tell you, she got teased unmercifully for calling it soda by one of our classmates we grew up with," Lucy explains, fluffing one of the pillows behind her so she can sit against the headboard.

Jesus, I just noticed Grace even has a fancy headboard! I glance over my shoulder at my mattress. I'm lucky to even have a box spring and an old wood bed frame.

Grace sticks her tongue out at Lucy. "Whatever. It didn't force me to back down. I stand by my appropriate knowledge and use of the English language. It's *soda*," she states emphatically while crossing her arms in defiance.

"Okay then, do you want a *soda* pop?" I tease, giving Grace a pointed look, the term sounding distinctly foreign as it rolls off my tongue.

"Yeah, sure. I'll have a soda, thank you very much." Then she turns to Lucy. "Large Hawaiian?"

Lucy nods. "We'll split a Hawaiian pizza. Remember how Kelsie got us hooked on them our freshman year?"

I notice Grace nodding her head with a sigh of remembrance as I make a gagging noise, turning toward Emmett, who shrugs.

"Trust me, bruh. I tried to explain to them that Hawaiian pizza is an abomination, but so far I haven't gotten that through their thick skulls."

He loops an arm around Lucy's neck from behind and

gives her a loving noogie with his knuckles. She squirms and shrieks. My gaze lands back on Grace rolling her eyes.

"Let me get this straight," I say to Grace, crossing my arms over my chest to imitate her, and shaking my head in disbelief. Her dark brown eyes land on my biceps and flash with something, but it quickly disappears. "So you have a problem with the term *pop*, but you dare to put pineapple on a pizza? Between your rearranging my organized chaos and your pizza choices, I'm not sure this roommate situation is going to work out."

I return my attention to the app and add their pizza choice to the order, requesting additional pepperoni on the pizza for Emmett and me.

"You guys want to watch a movie when the pizza arrives?" Lucy asks, giving me a pleading look before she turns to her friend. "We can celebrate your first night in the house!"

I groan. Not only am I exhausted, but I have a ton of stuff to do. I'd rather play my video games and go to bed early. But Lucy knows I can never say no to her when she puts on that ridiculous cherub angel expression.

"Tell your girl to stop making the face," I say to Emmett with a grumble.

Emmett laughs. "Yeah, it works on me too. Come on, dude. We'll watch something good like *Top Gun*."

"Fine. How about you, roomie?" I ask Grace, who looks as excited about a movie as I do.

"Fine," she says with a giant sigh, closing her laptop and setting it on her very uncluttered bedside table before jumping off the bed. "But there better be a bucket of butter popcorn and M&Ms with my name on it."

My head whips in her direction. "Do you eat your popcorn with M&Ms?"

"*Maybeee*," she replies cautiously, raising an eyebrow. "Why?"

"I may be able to tolerate you after all." I give her a sly grin and head toward the door to our room. Gesturing with a gentlemanly hand toward the stairs, I move out of the way and allow Grace to go out first.

"After you, *soda pop*."

"Where'd you come up with that one, genius?" she asks, brushing past me with a snort.

It's then I get a whiff of her perfume. She smells like summertime and lavender.

Why does this infuriating woman have to smell so good? I run a hand over my face as I follow her downstairs.

"I can read, you know. I noticed *The Outsiders* on your bookshelf."

She stops short and turns around on the stairs, giving me an appraising glance.

"I'll believe it when I see it," Grace chides sarcastically, spinning back around before flying down the stairs, leaving me staring after her without a witty comeback.

This is going to be a very long school year.

Chapter Three

G race

The first day of my junior year starts off with a giant-sized tornado that wakes me at the butt crack of dawn.

I bolt upright in a panic when I hear a loud thud coming from somewhere in the darkened room, followed by a roar of an expletive.

"Fuckin hell, that hurt!"

It's not even fully light out yet, the shadows still marking the bedroom with dark patches. Even so, when I glance over to Killian's side of the room, I can see the large shape looming nearby. My eyes pop wide when I see him hopping around the floor, holding a foot in the air.

"What the hell are you doing, dude?" I grouse, rubbing the sleep from my eyes and pushing myself up on an elbow. "Some of us were sleeping."

His body contorts in some kind of awkward dance like he's walking on hot coals... without a shirt on. He's dancing around *half-naked*.

Whoa.

I blink a few times trying to adjust to the low light and notice Killian is only wearing a low-hanging pair of sweats. That's it. Bare feet. Bare chest. A whole lot of football-playing muscles on display. I swallow thickly and try to look away. Try being the operative word.

He groans, finally dropping down on the edge of his bed, crossing a leg over his knee and rubbing his big toe. I do not notice the way his biceps bulge spectacularly with each movement.

Nope, I don't notice at all.

"I stubbed my toe on this goddamn dresser! It hurts, goddammit." Then he stops and glares at me, pointing an accusatory finger with his free hand at me. "And you're to blame."

I suck in a breath and my bottom lip between my teeth to hide my amusement. I mean, it is kind of funny to hear this ginormous football player—who gets pummeled on the regular by other ginormous players—curse and whine over a bump on his toe. The big baby.

I flop back onto my pillow and turn my head to face him. I will myself to not admire all the broad, chested masculinity on display just a few feet away from my bed and focus on his grumpy expression.

The sad truth is I've never been in the presence of a naked guy before. Or even half-naked.

It's not that I haven't dated guys or fooled around, because I have. I've had fun kissing and making out with plenty of guys at frat parties and whatnot. Even fumbled around in the back of the car with a boy in high school out in the middle of a country field. But I've never been fully naked with a guy. So Killian's near-nakedness at the moment is enough to shut me up as I stare in amazement and wonder at the male specimen before me.

Killian literally has a killer body. Is that how he got his nickname of Killer?

I've never asked where the name came from. I assumed he got it because of how he plays out on the football field.

But right now, he's doing a fine job of killing me with those ridged abs that ripple like an accordion when he bends low to examine his toe. The muscles in his back flex and tighten, as do his biceps that seem to strain against the taut skin of his arms.

He's quite the male specimen indeed.

Scientifically speaking, that is.

Killer suddenly looks up, his eyes catching mine, and he gives me a boyishly charming grin.

"You get your fill, soda pop? Or do I need to pose for you too?" He crooks his elbow and pops his bicep muscle in a ridiculous body-builder flex.

I make a squeaking noise and yank the sheet over my face, closing my eyes in embarrassment.

Killian chuckles, jumping over to my bedside and tugs the covers from my grip.

"Stop it, you beast!" I wail and whine, trying to wiggle the sheet free to cover my eyes again. "Let me go back to sleep."

"You seem wide awake to me," he says knowingly. "You might as well get used to it now because you'll be seeing a lot of *this* every day. I am not shy about my body."

I peek an eye out from under my protection and see him

twirl in a circle, running a hand down his chest and in the direction of his...OMG. He's pulling a Magic Mike on me.

Killian does that stomach roll thing that male strippers do, making a lewd *Boom-chic-a-wow-wow* sound as he lowers his hand in his pants.

"Oh, my God! You're so gross!" I shout, flipping over to face the other direction and chastise myself for even caring.

Killian snickers and I know he's just trying to get under my skin and get me flustered. And doing a damn good job of it, I might add.

Rude and disgusting or not, Killian is right about one thing. I will be seeing a lot of him and his body in the coming days, weeks, and months. So either I pull up my big girl panties and get used to it or come up with another solution to the predicament of too much exposure to my roommate's body parts.

Just then, a brilliant plan pops into my head. Smiling discreetly against the pillow, I know exactly what I'll do later to ensure that privacy and decency can be restored.

* * *

The last lecture of the day ends at four-thirty. I'm feeling tired after my interrupted sleep this morning as I blindly follow the other students up the stairs and out of the auditorium-sized classroom. Most everyone is looking down at their phones and others are chatting about the class or catching up from the summer.

I was going to stick around and talk to Dr. Hang Su, the professor of the mobile software engineering course I've been excited about taking since I started at CFU, but decide to wait until our next class on Thursday in favor of going to get some much-needed caffeine at the student center and cafe on my way home.

This year I get to start the upper level courses in my computer science engineering major and I'm so excited about the aspects of designing software systems and applications.

Math and science have always come easy to me. Maybe that's because I have parents who were both tech giants in their own right. My dad was the lead designer for the tech company he co-owned with my uncle in San Francisco. And my mom is the COO of a software development company that has branches in the US, China, and the UK. To say it's in my blood is an understatement.

As I get to the top of the landing, a familiar voice stops me from behind. I turn around and see the grinning face of one of my lab partners from freshman year, Marco Kelly.

"Hey, Grace! I was hoping we'd be in the same classes this year," Marco says, throwing his arms around me in an awkward hug as we enter the main corridor of the computer science building. I stiffen and he pulls back.

Marco also happens to be a guy I went out with a few times—and kissed once—but who hasn't gotten the hint I'm not into him.

"Oh, hey, Marco." I say, giving him a small smile as I fidget with the strap of my backpack in the hallway of Morton Hall as students move around us like water around river rocks.

Marco is a super nice guy and we hung out a lot over the last two years as friends, playing video games or working on assignments together. Marco is not a bad-looking guy or lacking in the intelligence or ambition department.

What he is lacking is that *thing*. The thing that gets me

excited to be around him. Some people call that chemistry or zing or zip. Whatever it is, he doesn't do it for me.

"How was your summer? Did you go anywhere fun? How's the ranch?"

Since we spent a lot of time together, Marco knows a lot about me and my life off campus. It isn't as if I don't like him, I just don't like him the way he apparently likes me.

I'm about to answer his questions when he starts into this monologue about what he did over the break.

"You won't believe it, but I attended that summer program in L.A. with NASA and we designed robots that will be used on a future trip to Mars. Isn't that amazing?"

"That's cool." I nod my head and smile politely, not really listening as he continues to bore me with the details.

Now I remember another thing Marco was lacking—the social skills to hold a conversation with someone in real life. He has verbal diarrhea of the mouth.

And then suddenly, out of nowhere, my feet lift off the floor and strong arms are wrapped securely around my waist as I am jiggled back and forth like a rag doll.

"Ahhh!" I let out a piercing shriek and Marco's eyes bulge out incredulously like he's watching Godzilla attack a woman.

"Hey there, soda pop! Whatcha doing?"

Oh. My. God. It's my annoying roommate using that also annoying nickname he finds so hilarious.

What is it with men using nicknames for me? First my dad and now Killian? Do they find it too hard to call me Grace? Or even Gracie like Lucy and Kelsie do?

My feet once again touch the ground and I shift to regain my balance. When I glance at Marco, his head is craned up to stare at the hulking presence of Killian.

It's kind of amusing to see the look of horror on Marco's face.

Killian centers himself between me and Marco, smiling congenially back and forth between us.

Finally, since no one seems to be saying anything, he introduces himself to the staring, tongue-tied Marco.

"Yo, bro. I'm Killer." He reaches a bear-sized hand out to Marco, who shakes it with his long, thin, gamer hands. "Are you Gracie's boyfriend?"

Killian glances at me curiously when I can't control the burst of laughter that spews from my mouth. I slap a hand over my lips, trying to stifle it and gurgle in embarrassment.

"No, um, we're just friends. Killian, this is Marco Kelly. Marco, meet my..." Oh shit, how the heck do I introduce him? Is Killian my friend? Do I just say he's my roommate?

I'm sure to anyone else, the fact that I'm roommates with a CFU football player will seem very strange. It's still crazy even to me.

But Killer takes the reins on introductions when he throws an arm over my shoulder and makes sure there is no room for question about how we know each other.

"Roommate," Killian gushes proudly. "Me and Grace are new bunkmates. Aren't we, soda pop?"

Marco blanches and takes a noticeable step back. My mouth gapes open as I try to explain and clarify. "Uh..."

"Oh, that's cool," Marco replies quickly, the confusion clear in the frown of disapproval on his face. "But I thought you and Kelsie were still roommates?"

I shake my head, trying to hide the irritation I still feel over Kelsie leaving me high and dry, resulting in this uncomfortable new living arrangement.

It's more of a sadness really. A feeling of abandonment that hit me like a high-speed train and crushed me under the weight of it. Thankfully, my dad helped me see that Kelsie leaving had nothing to do with me or our friendship. It was just a great opportunity she couldn't pass up and wasn't because she didn't like me anymore.

It was nothing like the reason my mom left us. She left for more selfish reasons. Like not wanting to be a full-time mom to me.

"No, Kelsie was in Paris for the summer and is now studying abroad this semester. She comes back in January. So I'm living off campus in the same house as Lucy and her boyfriend." I don't dare look up at Killian, but I feel him stiffen.

"And me!" he adds, squeezing my shoulder with his warm hand. When I steal a glance up at him, he flashes a triumphant smile. "You lucky girl."

Argh. Lucky only if I can figure out a way to smother this dude in his sleep without getting caught.

Marco seemingly gets the message Killian is obviously sending—the one that says *back off, bro*—and he checks his phone.

"Well, listen, I gotta go pick up some dinner before my study session tonight. I'll see ya round, Grace." He turns too quickly and nearly trips over his own feet before nervously waving at us over his shoulder. Then in a voice terse and strained, he says, "You too, Killian."

I can both feel and hear Killian's deep, thunderous chuckle. I swing an arm and playfully punch him in his stomach and am met with a hard block of concrete.

"Ahh, it was so fun to meet your friend, Gracie!" Killer says in a sing-song voice, grabbing hold of my hand and swinging it as we walk down the hallway together. "You should invite him over for a sleepover because that dude wants nothing more than to get into your bed."

My face flares red with both indignation and embarrassment.

That's it.

Now I'm more resolved than ever to hang up that curtain I ordered online this morning to divide our room in half. We need a clear barrier between us if this is going to work.

Because this boy needs to learn boundaries.

Chapter Four

K illian

"What the hell is this thing?"

My voice is thunderous as I stand in the doorway of my shared bedroom, staring indignantly at a giant curtain hanging across the length of the room.

It's a bright pink and green divider covered with a floral print that wasn't there when I left this morning. I hate it at first sight.

"Isn't it great?" Grace's cheerful voice calls out from somewhere behind the divider, which may as well be the Berlin wall.

"A curtain?" I stammer, stepping into the room to examine it more closely. "Why?"

I admit, Grace's rearrangement of my things on the first day may have been over the top and might have thrown me for a loop, but I hope she doesn't find me difficult to live with. I think she's cool, even if a bit too tidy. And let's not forget she's easy on the eyes too.

But this thing is ridiculous and has to go. I kind of like seeing her snuggled up in her bed in the morning.

The curtain is suddenly thrown open and Grace's head pops through. Her disembodied head reminds me of the "here's Johnny" scene from the horror movie *The Shining*. I almost jump back out of fright.

"You don't like it?" she asks, a slight frown playing on her lips.

I stare at those lips a little longer than I should, wondering how they'd feel against mine, but shake the thought away as I rub a hand down my face and let out a groan. "I don't get it. Am I that hideous?"

She shrugs and a hand emerges from the curtains and pokes my abdomen. "Yep, one hundred percent hideous. All those abs...ewww!" she squeals and pokes her head back behind the curtain.

I laugh. "Oh that's it, soda pop!" I throw back the curtain and chase after her, which is really only three steps to her bed. I pick her up—she's lighter than a bag of feed— and toss her onto her bed where she bounces once and giggles. I pin her arms above her head with one hand and tickle her with the other.

Her laughter intensifies and I know I've found her weakness. Just underneath her ribs. BINGO.

"Stop!" she pleads between fits of laughter, squirming in an attempt to get away. But she's no match for my size and weight so her resistance is futile.

"Say uncle!" I cajole, continuing my tickle attack. It's what I always do with my younger brothers except, in this case, my body has a very different response to Grace's lithe frame underneath me.

And her scent this up close and personal is intoxicating. I shouldn't notice how good she smells, right? We both stop for a beat and stare at each other. I swallow. It started off as fun and now it's moved into a whole different territory.

Shit, Grace is...no, no, this is my roommate. She is abso-fucking-lutely OFF LIMITS.

Maybe this curtain idea of hers has merit after all. I definitely need some distance because my body is reacting in a way it shouldn't be for my friend and roommate.

I'm about to jump off her bed when I hear Lucy screech loudly behind me. I turn to find her holding the curtain in one hand and staring at us with wide eyes.

"What's going...on here?" Lucy's voice breaks off as Grace and I both freeze, immediately pulling away from each other like we're made of hot lava.

"Oh, hey, Lucidity, what's up?" I say, trying to sound as casual as possible, like nothing inappropriate was just happening, calling her by the nickname I gave her last year. It was one of those long nights of heavy drinking when she was making zero sense, but claimed she did.

Lucy's gaze ping-pongs from me to Grace and then back to me.

"I thought I heard Grace yell." Her lips twist in confusion.

Grace laughs and throws a pillow at me. I chuck it back at her and it hits her in the head with a soft thud and she falls back onto her bed.

"Geesh, Killer. Don't kill my friend," Lucy admonishes and smacks me against the chest as she walks by toward Grace.

"What in the world was going on in here anyway? You guys looked like you were getting busy."

Grace laughs. Hard. Like that's so improbable?

"We were just having a lively disagreement over our new room accessory here." Grace motions to the curtain like she's a game show host. "Because Killian doesn't approve of this perfect solution to the privacy issue that has recently come to light. Behold, our new room divider."

Lucy runs a hand over the colorful and very girly fabric. "I mean...they are, uh, intense."

I point in agreement. "Aha! See? I'm not the only one who thinks these are ridiculous."

Grace shrugs. "I think they're perfect. This way I don't have to see any of the goings-on over on your side of the room." Her words seemed rushed and it further confuses me.

"What goings-on? So you saw a little show. Nothing you haven't seen before, I'm sure."

Grace gives me an annoyed glare and snorts. "And what happens when you want to bring one of your skanky-skanks up here? I definitely do not want to see that!"

Hmm...she might have a valid point.

We haven't discussed the protocol for when either or both of us might want to have company spend the night in the future. It was easy when I lived with Emmett because I could just kick him out for a few hours, and he understood and gave me space when needed. But I have a feeling Grace might not be as willing to get lost during those post-party evenings when I want to get it on with a girl.

Grace's smile dims slightly before she changes the subject and turns to Lucy. "How was your advanced biochemistry class today?"

Lucy shrugs. "Better than organic chem, that's for sure. That class sucks a bag of dicks."

"Wow! It must really be awful if you don't like it. You're our in-house science queen."

"Do you have Professor Pelensky?" I ask, grabbing my desk chair and straddling it backwards, arms crossed over the chair back.

Lucy's eyes widen as she stares at me like she can't believe what she just heard. "How did you know that?"

I suddenly feel self-conscious. I'm sort of a closet science nerd, but no one knows it. Even Emmett and Hendy aren't really aware of how smart I actually am.

To them, I'm just the big, dumb farm boy from Iowa who can eat a whole pizza in under three minutes, and only here for entertainment purposes. I prefer to keep them believing that.

I don't know if it's the idea that I have something just to myself or if I'm slightly embarrassed that I do have something to offer people other than a good time. Either way, I decide now's not the time to show my cards.

Last time I did that, I was in high school and my teammates made fun of me for the entire season. I had to do some jackass things to win back my status as the fun-loving jock with no brain cells. I'm not sure why it bothered me so much at the time. Maybe I just wanted to fit in.

Clearing my throat, I make up a plausible excuse. "Oh, I must've heard some chicks talking about that professor in the student union. That's all."

"Oh," Lucy replies, seemingly appeased before she turns back to Grace, clearly having lost interest in the line of questioning. "So, are you studying tonight or do you want to go out?"

Grace glances back at her computer. "Honestly, I have a shit ton of assignments already. Let's just go out this weekend."

Lucy nods. "Alright. I should probably study too. See you kids later," she says, giving us a wave.

But then at the last minute, she stops and glances over her shoulder. She signals with her fingers from her eyes to the two of us. "I'll be watching you two. No funny business."

She laughs before closing the door on us. When I look back at Grace, I catch her staring at me with a flash of something I can't read in here yes. She quickly turns away and grabs her laptop. "I need to study," she says, flopping down on her bed. The space between us is suddenly filled with an awkward silence.

"Right. I'll just be on my side of the room," I state dryly, yanking the curtains closed behind me with a *snick*.

I know I should get to work on my independent project because the research time alone is going to take an eternity. Because I have such personal reasons for taking this project on, not only for the grade aspect, and I need to give it one-hundred percent of my attention.

Deciding that my focus would be better suited if my desk were turned away from the wall, I rearrange my work-space by moving the desk. This also serves the dual purpose of keeping the likes of little Miss Peeper from snooping and from getting an eyeful of what I'm working on. Not that she would care, but I don't need her to know what's going on with my family's business.

Satisfied with the changes, I sit down and boot up my computer, reminding myself that time's a-wastin' and I can't afford to get sidetracked with my computer games. I have to force myself to concentrate and not fuck around on the internet.

I pop in my earbuds and turn on some music so I can drown out the clickity-clacking tapping of Grace's keyboard on her side of the room. I don't have the time to wonder what she's doing right now.

After a few minutes, my curiosity gets the best of me. On impulse, I glance toward the divider and can just make out the outline of her body silhouetted by the bedside lamp. And that, of course, has me remembering how good it felt to be on top of her, pinning her arms above her head and tickling her belly. The way the fabric of her shirt had ridden up just enough so that I could feel her smooth skin beneath it. I even felt a little scar there. I ponder what the scar could be from before forcing myself to re-focus on my paper.

* * *

I'm not sure how long I've been working, but it's dark outside now, the only light in the room coming from my desk lamp and Grace's lamp behind the curtain. I stretch and reach for my water bottle. Downing the last of it, I decide it's time to brush my teeth and call it a night.

With my AirPods still in and the loud wail of heavy metal music filling my ears and drowning my thoughts, I make my way to the bathroom door that adjoins our bedroom. I resist the urge to glance in Grace's direction when I pass by the curtain and instead turn the handle of the door that jiggles a little and push it open.

Everything freezes the moment I look up and see...her.

Grace is stepping out of the shower dripping wet and, with a shriek of surprise, she desperately tries to cover herself with a towel. But it's too late. I've already gotten an eyeful.

"Killer! What the hell? Get the fuck out of here!"

With the music still loud in my ears, I can only see the movement of her mouth and don't really hear what she's saying. Even if I could, my focus is on the freshly showered and naked roommate in front of me, not on her words.

Holy shit. This woman is fucking beautiful.

With a slow perusal, I notice a small half-moon scar on her abdomen, the one I felt earlier. Maybe she had some kind of surgery?

My eyes move up to her breasts that are damned near perfection. My hands are big and her tits would be a handful.

She's tiny, but strong with an athletic body that's lean from maybe running or yoga.

There is no doubt I will jerk off to this image in the future.

One perfect woman to rule them all.

"What did you just say?" Grace says, wrapping the towel tighter and then gesturing with her hand for me to move. "And will you stop gawking and leave?"

"Huh?" I ask, still a little dazed, but shield my eyes with my hand and bend my head downward so I only see her bare feet. They are small and cute too.

"Did you just say, 'one perfect woman to rule them all'?"

My eyes pop back up to hers. Oh shit. Did I say that out loud?

Deny, deny, deny.

My gaze lands on her face, which is flushed pink. Maybe from the hot shower or from me seeing her naked. But it makes me want to reach out and touch the soft lines of her face. Run a hand down her pert nose. Trace the curve of her collarbone where water droplets still rest.

Grace fidgets under the weight of my stare as she tries unsuccessfully to keep the towel from slipping from where she's managed to hold it above her chest. Those perfect breasts come back into view. Fuck me.

I look away again and grab my toothbrush and feign

ignorance, tugging the earbuds out of my ear. "Oh, no. I was just singing along to a song."

"Oh, you're listening to music," she states as her own slow, interested gaze travels down my torso. I'm wearing only my track pants and no shirt and enjoy the fact that she's not as unaffected as I thought.

I'm surprised she hasn't kicked me out yet. I want to see how long she'll let me stay, so I add some toothpaste to my toothbrush and start brushing my teeth at the sink.

With a mouthful, I turn my head to respond. "Sorry, I didn't hear the shower. Why didn't you lock the door?"

She sighs. "I did, you oaf. But I think it's broken. Old door." She pauses and then reaches in front of me to grab her hairbrush as if it's the most natural thing in the world that we're side by side in the bathroom together. I watch her in the steamy mirror as she holds the knotted towel with one hand and then strokes the brush through her long wet hair.

"Uh, we should probably implement a policy on knocking or something. I mean, this was bound to happen at some point, but we don't need to make a habit of it."

Bummer. I wouldn't mind that.

"Yeah. Probably. That makes sense," I manage to say with a mouth full of toothpaste.

Although we both agree to ensure each other's bathroom privacy in the future, I don't make a move to leave the room and she doesn't insist. Instead, we stand in front of the double sinks, me brushing my teeth and her combing through her hair. She glances at me from the corner of her eye.

"What?" she asks curiously, setting the brush down on the countertop and then reaching for a bottle of lotion. My thoughts immediately go somewhere they shouldn't.

I spit out the remaining toothpaste and croak out a response. "Nothing."

Grace stands there for a second, crossing her arms over her breasts, which only accentuates the plumpness under the towel. I stare back. She taps a foot on the floor and raises an eyebrow.

"Do you mind? I have to change."

"Go right ahead," I tease, gesturing with a hand as I lean against the countertop. "Don't let me stop you."

She lets out an aggrieved sound and pushes against my bare chest with her palms. It does nothing to move me, but I let her do it because I like the feel of her hands on me. They are soft and warm.

"Argh! Go away now!"

I chuckle and slowly back out of the bathroom. She slams the door behind me with a huff as I head back into the bedroom, yelling over my shoulder, "Just let me know if you need any help with that lotion!"

A few minutes later, I hear the bedroom door open and the sound of her rummaging in a drawer. Then the sound of her climbing onto her mattress, sheets rustling and the metal creak of the bedsprings. With her lamp on and the curtain shut blocking off my view, all I can see is her curvy silhouette before she lies down on the bed and turns the light off.

Her fresh, feminine scent fills the room and I breathe in deeply, my hands clasped behind my head on the pillow.

"Killer?" Grace asks quietly a few minutes later. "Are you still awake?"

"Yeah?" I stretch out on my full-size bed, rolling my ankles, my feet sticking off the end of the bed. At home I have a twin, which is way too small for my size, but even this bed makes me feel like a giant. I wish I could have gotten a queen mattress up here.

"Did you see anything...you know, earlier in the bathroom?" she asks.

I smirk up at the ceiling, knowing full well I did get a glimpse. "Nope."

"Are you lying?"

"Nope." I cross my fingers and smile to myself, wondering what she's doing on her side of the room.

"Are you sure you aren't lying?" Her voice is laced with annoyance and something about that is endearing, like she really does care what I think even if she won't admit it.

I laugh. "Define lying. Because I didn't see anything I didn't already know was there."

"Oh, God! That's so embarrassing," she whispers and I can hear her flop over on her bed.

"Why are you embarrassed?" I roll to my side and prop my head on my hand.

"Because...you like saw me practically naked." The image of her body fills my mind and I reach down to adjust myself. I cannot get hard thinking about my roommate.

"I've seen naked girls before," I manage.

There's a pause and I shift to the other side on the bed, listening for her to respond. It's kind of fun to talk to her even though I can't see her face. Knowing what I already know of her, she's probably blushing.

"I don't doubt that," she grumbles. "But please knock in the future before just barging in like a caveman. And fix that lock."

"Okay. I'll do that this weekend. But, Grace?"

"Yeah."

"There's nothing to be embarrassed about. You're beautiful," I add, remembering all the gorgeous curves of her breasts, toned abs, and slender legs on display.

Grace is quiet for a moment and I wonder if I overstepped. I don't mean to embarrass her any further. I'm just stating facts.

She is fucking hot. And if I can make it through this year without pulling my hair out, it will be a miracle.

"You're not too shabby yourself, Killer," Grace replies almost reluctantly. It makes me smile and I flip back over to my back.

"Goodnight, soda pop," I whisper.

"Goodnight, Killian," she whispers back.

I close my eyes and drift off to sleep listening to the small puffs of Grace's breath on the other side of The Great Divide.

Chapter Five

G race

Over the last two weeks, I keep having the same recurring dream about a bear.

The dream starts out the same way each time. I'm camping in the forest with my dad, or sometimes Lucy, but when I wake up in the dream, I'm alone and lost in the wilderness.

The thick trees swallow me up as I walk through the darkened forest looking for our campsite. I yell out, "Hello, where are you? Help me! I'm lost." But no one else is around to hear me or to help.

It's then that I hear growling and snorting, scuffling around the leaf-lined floor of the forest. I search around and see a brownish figure off behind some shrubs and trees, lumbering around in search of food or scratching its big hairy body against the bark of a Douglas Fir.

From a distance, the bear seems totally cool. Like a big teddy bear. But I keep my distance, trying to remain as quiet as I can to avoid detection, just watching to see what he does. The bear finally notices me as I do my best to crouch and hide. Of course my presence piques his interest and he closes in on me, his brown snout sniffing the air at my scent.

I remember the instructions given in Girl Scouts that when confronted by a bear, you're supposed to look as large and menacing as you possibly can. So I raise my arms in the air and roar as loud as I can manage.

The bear stops long enough to give me an odd look. I glance down to see what has grabbed his interest and realize I'm not wearing any clothes.

I'm naked and the bear is staring at me like I'm a snack.

The bear looms his large, hairy bear body above me, blocking out what little light there was from the moon above. And then the weight of his paws land on top of my shoulders and I'm being shaken like I'm a martini tumbler. I'm going to die!

"Grace...Gracie...wake up."

Why is a bear talking? Bears can't talk.

"SODA POP!"

My eyes fly open, my heart racing like a sprinter on a race track, and I blink. And then scream.

"Bear!"

Suddenly, I'm awake and realize where I'm at and who is hovering over me with his hands on my shoulders.

It's not a bear at all. It's just my roommate.

Killian's loud snorts of laughter could wake the whole damn house. I slap my hand over his mouth to muffle his noisy sounds, feeling his broad grin grow against my palm.

"Shhh...be quiet. You're going to wake up Emmett and Lucy downstairs."

I know they can hear us up here because we've heard them several times in the last week getting it on. Good grief, they are loud when they fuck.

I pull my hand away as Killian plunks down on the edge of my bed, slipping his hand under my hips to scooch me over to make room for his gigantic self.

He scoffs. "Me? I'm not the one screaming in my sleep."

The telltale sign of the nightmare drips down from my temple, the beads of sweat congregating at my hairline. I flick them away with my finger and turn my head away, mumbling my apology into my pillow.

"Sorry. I didn't mean to wake you up."

Killian's finger notches underneath my chin and he swivels my head back to face him. It's then I notice the worry etched in his brow.

"Hey, it's fine. But are you okay?" He glances out the window above the bed, the soft light of sunrise barely peeking through. "I'm on duty at the ag center this morning before I have my scheduled weight training. Are you gonna be okay, though?"

I wave off his concern, which is sweet but unnecessary. "Oh, for sure. It's no biggie."

He chuckles. "I don't know. Sounded big to me. You yelled 'bear.'"

I avoid his gaze when suddenly the sheet is whipped from over my legs and Killian leans over me, as if in search of something.

"Oh, my God," I yelp, shivering from the abrupt loss of warmth. "What the hell are you doing?"

Killian lifts his shoulders and hands the top sheet back to me, one of my legs still poking out.

"Just checking to make sure you didn't pee the bed," he says matter-of-factly. "My youngest brother, Jamie, used to have accidents in the middle of night from nightmares. He would secretly hide behind the couch when I was watching horror movies. He thought I didn't know it, but I did. The problem was he'd end up peeing his bed in the middle of the night from a scary nightmare. Then he'd come into my room reeking of piss and I would have to change his sheets before our parents woke up."

"Oh, poor kid."

"Pfft," he huffs. "The little shit did it all the time until he was probably nine or ten."

I furrow my brows. "Then why didn't you stop him from watching?"

Killian looks thoughtfully out the window, seemingly thinking this obvious suggestion through. "I don't know. I kinda liked that he felt he could rely on me to be there to protect him when he needed it."

My heart squeezes. How can this big oaf of a football player, all tough and huge, be such a caring, gooey teddy bear on the inside?

"That's really sweet. You're a good brother." I toy with the edge of the sheet and breathe in the clean, masculine scent of the guy sitting so close to me. He's so warm, I want to snuggle up next to him and get closer. The air seems to crackle and spark and suddenly I'm hot. *Everywhere.*

I throw the covers off my legs, realizing too late that I'm only in an oversized T-shirt and panties.

Killian's gaze lands on my thighs and I clench them together tightly. Then he nudges my bare knee with his elbow, which is covered with the long sleeve of his flannel. He has on his Carhartt work clothes—the ones I insisted he must wash after every use because they stink of cow manure and the odor permeates our room.

I don't usually see him in these clothes because he's always up and gone by the time I wake up for my first class.

If there's one thing I have to say about Killian Palmer, it's that he is one dedicated guy. He has a great work ethic. He loves working at the agricultural center and has told me some funny stories about the farm animals there, especially the cow named Old Bessie who is pregnant.

I haven't corrected him yet, but he seems to be under the impression that I'm just a city girl who knows nothing about farms or ranches. And maybe I don't know as much as he does about it, but I do know my way around a barn and ride horses on the regular when my dad tends to the cattle.

Killian stands up and shakes his head. "I miss those shit-heads sometimes. But I'll admit, rooming with you is definitely better than sharing a room with either Mac or Jamie."

"Ahhh...did you just pay me a compliment?"

Killian scoffs and grabs his bag from the floor near his bed, flinging the curtain back as he heads to the door.

"It's not hard to be a better roommate than those two fools." He shoots me a pointed look. "And when I give you a real compliment, you'll know it. I promise you that."

Then he winks and before he shuts our bedroom door behind him, I get a good look at his ass in those Wranglers.

I flop back down on the mattress with a sigh. There's no way I'm going to fall back to sleep now without dreaming about a sweet Golden Retriever roommate who has a great ass.

Chapter Six

K illian

Giggles.

Drunken giggles echo on my side of the bedroom, turning me even more surly than I've been in a long time. All because I was the reason we lost the football game tonight.

It was our first home game and we were tied up in the fourth quarter. Hendy passed me the ball at the fifty-yard-line. I caught it in the air, spun around, and the next thing I knew, out of nowhere, I got pummeled by the opposing team's right tackle and the ball flew from my hands like my grip was made out of butter. The ball was tossed into the air and the opposing player made a successful grab for it and then ran it into the end zone for a touchdown. On my fucking fumble!

So instead of going out to the party at Hendy's on-campus frat house, I came home to sulk and pout, and play video games all night.

I'm not usually this serious or uptight about football—or life. I'm normally the guy making everyone laugh and having a good time.

But I've been off lately and grouchier than ever. Probably because I haven't been laid in weeks.

That could have probably been remedied tonight if I went out to the party and found someone to hook up with, but the thought didn't entice me like it used to.

The thought of bringing a rando back to the house and having sex with her in the room that I share with Grace didn't sound appealing at all. In fact, it somehow felt wrong. Like it was a violation of our friendship and roomie agreement.

Which is why I opted to come home by myself. When I first got in and showered up, filling my belly with whatever I could scrounge up from the refrigerator, I planned on working on my research project. But ten minutes later, I was fast asleep, my head on my closed laptop that remained untouched.

I wake up when I hear the sound of the girls' laughter in the bed next to me. I remove my earbuds and look at the time. It's just after 10 p.m.

"The curtain isn't soundproof, ya know." I state my complaint grumpily and with some force to overcompensate for their noisy volume.

The curtain whooshes open and Lucy stands there, hoisting a can of some alcoholic beverage in the air.

"Since when did you become a party pooper? We're celebrating Grace's twenty-first birthday tonight. You have to come out with us, Killer. It's going to be lit!" she says, only instead of intelligibly, she slurs out the word birthday and it sounds like *flurfday*. She even spits a little, which is pretty funny. She wipes the spittle from her mouth with a flourish.

I hide my grin as Emmett walks in and glances between Lucy and me, turning to me with a sharp look.

"Dude, you better be getting ready to come out to help me with..." He motions to his girlfriend and then to Grace, who pops her head under Lucy's arm and then leans against her friend's shoulder. "These two drunken lunatics."

"Um, as tempting as it sounds, I'm staying in tonight. I'm not in a celebratory mood," I declare reluctantly. I point down at my computer screen. "I've got a shit ton of work to do for next week."

I sense a presence above the screen and glance up to find Grace standing there, giving me what can only be described as sad puppy dog eyes.

"Killer..." she whines, batting her long dark lashes at me. I swear to Christ, if she sat down on my lap right now and continued to look at me like that, I'd do anything for her. I swallow. "It's my birthday! You have to grant me a birthday wish and come out to have a drink with me!"

I give her a sheepish smile. I feel bad that I didn't know it was her birthday today. I guess I'm a shit roommate for not knowing. But honestly, I haven't been home much in the past week.

"Happy birthday, soda pop!" I smile, standing up to give her a hug. The top of her head comes up to the bottom of my chin. She snuggles in and, on unbalanced feet, she lolls against me. I chuckle. "Seems like the birthday girl has already done some pre-partying. Maybe you should drink some water before you go."

She grunts into my chest. "Water, schmahter." She

pouts and then tips her face up to look at me. "Come on, Killian. Come out with us just for a little bit. It'll be fun!"

I dislodge my hands from around her tipsy frame and let her go. She teeter-totters forward and with the grace only a drunk girl has, promptly trips over my backpack. The momentum has her toppling face first into me.

Because I'm not expecting it, she hits hard and I fall back into the chair where she collapses into my lap. I grab onto her hips and pull her snug against me so she avoids any further damage to life or limb.

For a long moment, neither of us moves. She feels tiny in my arms, but something about her here feels...right. It's a strange sensation that I've never felt before. Like going home. Only this isn't my home and Grace is just my roommate.

I let myself breathe in the scent of her shampoo. I feel the bare skin of her midriff against my forearm that's wrapped around her middle. Her skin dots with goose-bumps before she pushes a hand against my chest as if to distance herself.

"Oops!" she says, erupting into another fit of giggles. "My bad."

I glance at Emmett, who rolls his eyes. "Come on, dancing queen, we've gotta go." He offers a hand of assistance to Grace, who accepts it, standing and turning back around to me.

"You sure you don't want to come?"

"I'd love to, but I need to get this work done. I'm really sorry. Maybe we can grab dinner this week to celebrate. I'll buy you a soda pop at Duffy's Diner," I say with a wink.

Grace nods her head in acceptance and lets out another giggle. "I'm holding you to it."

"Have fun, kids," I add as the three of them head out the door just as loudly as they came in.

I open my laptop and try to refocus, slipping on my headphones and getting to work. But the more I research, the more I think about the family farm and the trouble I know my dad is having this year. It was all but confirmed when I heard from Mac earlier in the day.

Mac: You coming home for a visit soon?

Me: I just left.

Mac: Yeah, like three weeks ago.

Me: It's the start of the season. You know I can't just up and leave.

Mac: Oh. Right. K. It's just that it's not the same.

I frown and press the call button.

"What's up?" I ask because I hate beating around the bush.

"Nothing." He pauses and then sighs. "Dad's stressed. He's always upset over something and that's not like him. I'm worried, bro."

I feel every muscle in my body tighten like a vise grip. If it's noticeable to a teenage boy, then it's not great.

"I'm sure it's just business stuff and nothing for you to worry about," I assure him, but it's mostly to assure myself. Our Grandfather Hank died of a heart attack at age sixty-eight, and while my dad is only in his late forties, that possibility is always in the back of our minds.

"Yeah. I know. I just...anyhow, I gotta go. Annie is coming over later to have dinner with the fam. See ya."

I smile at the mention of his girlfriend. "Okay, bro. Have fun and don't worry so much."

"Yeah, yeah. Later," he says as the line goes silent.

The conversation brought even more anxiety into my chest. My gut tells me Mac's observations are right and something is going on with my dad. But my head tells me not to overreact and to find a way to help out the best I can from here.

This research project could be the thing to help my family's farm out. I promise myself that I'll check in this week with my dad and insert myself into the business affairs.

School and football are important, but my family always comes first.

* * *

I'm rifling through the refrigerator in the kitchen when I hear noises at the front door. I frown, trying to figure out what it is. It sounds like someone is trying to break in.

I slowly close the fridge and glance at the microwave clock. It's one-thirty in the morning.

"What the hell?" I mutter to myself, walking to the front door to investigate further. But when I peer through the window at the top of the door, there's nothing there. It's probably a raccoon. We get those little bandit-eyed critters all the time.

I turn to head back into the kitchen when I hear the noise again. Against my better judgment, I open the door, ready to reach down to snatch any animal trying to get in. What I'm not expecting to catch is...Grace.

"Well, hello there, sailor!" she says, her words slurring so it comes out as *ell, ello, there, sailo*. She steps backward and goes to lean against the front porch post and misses, tipping off balance. She overcorrects her footing and pitches forward, right into my arms.

She squirms with a laugh as I help her stand. When she wobbles again, I simply lift her off her feet and pick her up in my arms. She squeals, but wraps her legs around my waist, her arms clumsily thrown over my neck.

"You're like the size of a tree and I'm a squirrel!" she shrieks with goofy drunken laughter, as if it's the funniest thing she's ever said.

"Well, aren't you a happy drunk? I'm glad you had fun tonight." I tip my chin down to look at her face, her cheek pressed against my chest.

"You smell nice." She inhales a giant breath. "I like it better when you shower."

I can't help but laugh. "Yeah, okay. Thanks for the commentary. Now we need to get you food," I state, turning back around, my hands full of Grace's ass, and am about to shut the door behind us when I realize no one else is with her. I look around the porch in search of the crew she went out with and no one is there.

Why is Grace here by herself?

"Uh, where are Lucy and Emmett?" I ask, toeing the door closed and walking us back inside. I'm completely stunned they would just leave Grace alone to walk home from a bar by herself at nearly two in the morning.

"Probably fucking in a bathroom," she groans and then hiccups. Her hand slides down my back.

"I'm sorry, what?"

I set her on the kitchen counter and step back, boxing her in on either side with my hands on the counter.

"They were dancing...you know..." She tries to demonstrate the body roll, her arms flailing and then her chest slumping. "They were getting it *onnnn*...." She trails off and her eyelids grow heavy.

"And?"

Her eyelids pop open again. "I felt like a third wheel. So I left."

"Did you let them know you were leaving?" I ask.

"Nope," she replies, letting the *P* pop.

Fuck.

I pull out my phone. There's a text message from Emmett.

> Emmett: Have you seen Grace? She went to the bathroom and then disappeared. Lucy is freaking out.

> Me: I got her. She's here and safe.

> Emmett: Thank fucking God!

> Me: I got it from here. Keep having fun. I'll tuck in Miss Drunky-Drunkerkins with some food, water, and aspirin.

> Emmett: 10-4. Just know, Lucy might come in there tomorrow and kill Grace.

> Me: Sounds like a good time.

I put my phone back in my pocket and grab a sports drink that is a sure hangover cure. I also snag a slice of leftover pizza the guys ordered earlier tonight.

"Whatcha doin'?" Grace asks.

"Eat," I say as I hand her the slice.

She glares at me and crosses her arms. "You're so bossy!"

I take a deep breath and look up at the ceiling. This woman is killing me.

"Please eat, Grace." I finally manage to persuade her as I hold the slice in front of her mouth. She leans forward, her mouth opens, and she takes a bite.

She chews for a minute and cocks her head to one side as if considering something. Then she grabs the slice and practically inhales it.

"This shit is good," she says in between ravenous bites that don't seem remotely feasible for the size of her mouth.

I watch her lips as they move with every mouthful and a dozen dirty thoughts cross my mind. I look away. I can't be thinking about Grace like this right now.

"Drink this," I insist and hold out the beverage to her. She downs it and then looks at the bottle.

"Why do you guys have kids' Pedialyte?" she asks, her dark brows furrowing in confusion. "Do we have a child living in this house?"

I chuckle because only her drunken mind would think that.

"It's a solid hangover cure," I explain. Turning to the fridge, I grab a bottle of cold water and stuff it in my pocket. I hand her a paper towel to wipe her hands and then pick her up and toss her over my shoulder.

"What are you doing?" she yells, tapping on my back with her palm.

I slap her ass and she lets out an outraged curse. "Taking you up to your bed. Now hush up. Marcus is upstairs asleep and he's a beast if you wake him up."

That seems to subdue her as I carry her up the two flights of stairs to our room. I flop her backwards onto her bed and set the bottle of water on her nightstand. With half-lidded eyes and a small smile, she quietly observes me.

"Should we get you into something more comfortable?" I ask as I rummage in her drawers and pull out a t-shirt and some shorts and toss them at her.

She holds up her arms like a little kid. I shake my head. "Uh-uh. I'm not doing that. You're on your own there, missy," I mutter.

She makes a pouty face. "Lucy or Kelsie would do it for me. They'd tuck me in like a good roommate should."

Stuck in a moment of uncertainty, I wait her out. Maybe she'll just do it on her own and I won't be put in the position to undress and change my drunk roommate.

"Please?" Grace pleads, sitting up and twisting around so I can see the back of her shirt. It has a zipper. FML. "I can't reach it...it's too hard for me to take off."

I groan. "Fine."

I kneel on the bed next to her, holding my breath and willing myself not to breathe in her scent as my finger and thumb close around the metal zipper pull. I tug it down, closing my eyes to avoid looking at all that soft skin.

I've undressed plenty of women in my time, but only for the purposes of getting them naked and into my bed.

This is not one of those times.

Grace wiggles her arms through the arm holes and it's then that I realize she's not wearing a bra. FML. I turn my face away as she tugs the shirt over her head and I hold out the t-shirt for her to put on.

"Can you grab me—" Her face goes pale and her hand flies to her mouth. Shit!

I haul her into the bathroom and she holds back her hair out of her face while she launches herself at the toilet to vomit.

When she finishes, she sits back on her haunches and I offer her a towel to wipe her lips.

"Sorry," she whimpers.

"It's okay. It's been known to happen to me a few times." I hold out a hand to help her up to the sink where she washes her face and then brushes her teeth. She glances at the toilet again.

"I have to..." She motions to the toilet.

I nod and step out, closing the bathroom door behind me while she uses the privacy.

When she emerges, I can see she's sobered up a bit, her face back to a normal color with pink, rosy cheeks.

"I'm sorry," she squeaks. "I drank way too much tonight."

"Well, it was your twenty-first birthday, so it's kind of a tradition. But you should be more careful in the future," I scold.

"Gee, thanks for the advice, Dad. I know that..." she grumbles, sliding onto the mattress a bit more tentatively than usual. She pulls the covers up to her chin and sighs.

"Did you at least have fun?" I ask, sitting on the edge of the bed down near her feet. I'm keeping my distance from her, knowing how vulnerable she is being this drunk.

She nods with a soft smile. "It was fun. I always have fun with Lucy. She's my BFF. My ride or die. She knows everything about me and all my faults." Grace leans in and speaks in a conspiratorial whisper. "Everything except one teeny, tiny secret."

She sticks out her index finger and giggles.

"What's that?" I ask, now very curious what on earth she could be hiding.

A blush creeps over her face and she closes her eyes. "I've never told her I'm still a virgin."

The word *virgin* hangs in the air and her eyes pop open wide, like she can't believe she just said that. She promptly throws her hands over her mouth.

"You're a virgin?" I ask, suddenly jumping off the edge of the bed surprised by this news. I mean, she's always got guys hanging on her every word at every party. And there was that kid I met a few weeks ago from one of her classes. He had goo-goo eyes for her.

"Oh, shit...did I say that out loud?" she asks.

I nod, still baffled by her drunken confession.

How the hell is this woman still a virgin?

Chapter Seven

G race

Holy crap, did I just let the cat out of the bag?

Okay, bad timing on the use of the euphemism. Because obviously my kitty is still securely in the bag, if you know what I mean.

Killian just stands there in an awkward stunned silence, his jaw gaping open. A very unusual occurrence for him unless he's shoving a whole pizza in his mouth.

"Oh, my God. Please, please, please forget I just said that." I throw my arm over my face, a blush creeping like vines up my neck and into my cheeks. "I'm drunk and can't be held liable for the things I say and do."

He bends down and pats at my thigh over the blanket. "Hey, it's not a big deal. I don't care. I'm just kinda shocked is all."

I drop my arm and give him a hard glare, pointing at

him for added emphasis. "Don't you dare breathe a word of this to anyone, Killer. I mean it."

He holds up his hands in an *"I'm innocent"* gesture. "I won't. I promise. I swear."

There's a stretch of silence that falls between us. Not uncomfortable, but more reflective, I guess you could say. The word of his promise lingers in my thoughts. Promises don't mean much to me because they've been broken so many times before.

Killian clears his throat, tipping his head thoughtfully.

"But can I ask... why?"

I snort, sober enough now to hold a conversation. "Why do I want you to keep your mouth shut? Or why haven't I had my V-card punched yet?"

Killian chuckles. "Both, I guess."

I scoot up against the pillows at the headboard and pat the space next to me, leaving room for him to sit. It might seem like an odd conversation to have in my bed, but with Killian, I don't mind it.

Over the last month, I've gotten to know him as a funny, sweet, loyal guy. And aside from his continued messiness on his side of the room, he's a very respectful roommate. I'm beginning to appreciate the big oaf.

Killian lifts an eyebrow at my suggestion, but sits down next to me, his oversized body warming me up the instant he's stretched out next to me. His bare feet dangle over the bed frame. Sheesh, he's just a huge giant.

I nervously pick at the edge of my satin sheet, wondering where to even start with the reasons and explanation.

"I've dated guys, ya know. Some nice ones and a few who were complete dickheads." Killian laughs softly at this. "But it never felt right. And now that I'm in college, it's even more like an albatross. I just want to rip off the bandage and get it over with, you know?" I pull my knees up to my chest, wrapping my arms around my legs and tucking my chin in the crevice.

His tone is laced with gentle understanding and something in my heart beats wildly. "Gracie, there's not some right or wrong way to...uh...lose your virginity. No timetable or expiration date. You should do whatever you feel is right for you."

I give a half-hearted groan. "I know. But I'm twenty-one now. It's not like I'm saving myself for marriage. In fact, I don't even want a relationship. That's why I was hoping I'd find some rando to do it with tonight. But I couldn't go through with it. The guys I danced with were all just...ick." I shudder and then tilt my head up to face him. His gaze is filled with compassion and empathy. "Does that make me a weirdo?"

Unexpectedly, Killian sits back down next to me and throws an arm behind my shoulders and tucks me in close. I breathe in his spicy deodorant and soapy clean scent. It feels so nice, warm and comfortable like my grandmother's crocheted blanket.

"That's a loaded question because I've always thought you were a weirdo," he teases, knuckling over my hair. I playfully elbow him in the ribs and we both laugh.

He gently rests his chin on the crown of my head and I feel his whiskers brush against me. But I don't move from his embrace, instead I savor the moment.

"How old were you when you popped your cherry?" I ask, suddenly curious about his sex life. I'd heard some outrageous talk about Killian's scoreboard of rotating women over the past few years, but since we became roommates, he hasn't brought one girl home with him. I haven't caught him in the act once.

Well, except the day I came home early from class with a headache and I heard what I thought was him jerking off in our room. I could hear the low grunts and the slap of skin from behind the closed door. His breath grew ragged, the bed creaked underneath his movements, and then I heard him climax with a long groan.

It shocked me how turned on I was by the mere sounds of him doing it. I lay awake that night imagining what he looked like while he masturbated.

The wildly inappropriate image runs through my head and my body heats in response. It makes me wonder what he's like with girls in bed.

I can feel his body move when he shrugs his shoulder in response to my question. "Oh, you know...I've always been a chick magnet. Lost it at fourteen to Lisa Probst. She was two years older than me. Which only proves that I am a true lady-killer."

The buzz I have is still in full effect and this makes me laugh louder than intended, slapping a knee with hilarity.

"Ha! That's funny. You are *so* not..."

He snorts, nudging me in my side. "How would you know? I've got mad skills in bed, woman."

It has to be the alcohol and my level of inebriation right now otherwise I'd never continue this crazy personal and highly intimate discussion. I shouldn't want to know how Killian is with girls that he sleeps with.

But I keep running my mouth instead of shutting it up.

Straightening my shoulders, I twist around and prop myself up on my knees, pressing into his thigh.

"Okay, then. Tell me, *lady-killer*, how exactly do you know you've, ahem... satisfied a woman in bed." I use air quotes and scrunch my nose because I think he's sorely over-estimating and exaggerating his abilities in the sack.

An irresistibly devastating grin widens on his face and he lifts his brows in what could be viewed as a dare.

I swallow hard, but don't back down.

"Do you want me to show you?"

Wait, what? How did Killian just turn this on me?

He must see the sheer panic on my face and he laughs.

"If you must know, I am a ladies first kind of guy. I make sure she comes before I do."

My jaw drops. My mouth dries. My brain goes fuzzy.

And my panties go damp.

I lick my lips and swallow again.

Oh, shit. Oh, no. Don't do it. Don't ask. Don't go there.

I go there.

"What do you do to make her come?" My voice has lost its confidence and it quivers on the last word.

Like a shark in water who smells the scent of blood, Killian uses this to his advantage. His palm lands on my bare thigh, my eyes gravitating down to watch and wait for what it does. He lightly runs it back and forth like that *Karate Kid* guy does when he practices his wax on-wax off technique. Goosebumps prickle over my sensitized flesh. Every point of contact zaps like a live wire.

"Grace?"

My name is said so quietly it almost doesn't sound like he said it out loud. More of a whisper on the air.

"Yeah?"

He leans in a fraction of an inch closer. My stomach tightens with butterflies. Killian's hand comes to a rest and he pauses. Our breaths mingle between us and I'm suddenly feeling lightheaded, but not from the effects of the alcohol I drank.

No, this is all Killian.

"If you really want to lose your virginity, I'm happy to volunteer as tribute. Then I can show you..."

A light from the hallway suddenly bursts through the door, bathing us in its harsh brightness.

"Grace Leigh Ford, how dare you leave the bar without telling me!" An angry Lucy comes barreling into our room, Emmett on her heels.

My head whips toward her at the same time Killian scampers off the bed, his arms swinging wildly as they tangle up in the curtain.

The next thing I know, there's a loud snapping sound. When I turn to look, I find him sprawled out in a heap on the floor covered with the floral pink curtain. The only thing visible are his legs.

And then a now startled Lucy exclaims, "Holy shit! Were you guys just about to have sex?"

Chapter Eight

K illian

Fuck. My. Life.

I groan as I work to untangle the fucking curtain from around my legs, which proves more difficult than shoving a defensive tackle out of my way. Finally free of the stupid thing, I stand and covertly adjust my junk so no one notices the raging hard-on bulging in my pants.

"No," Grace squeaks in a most unconvincing tone at the same time I give a deep and resounding, "No?"

Lucy eyes us suspiciously and Emmett raises an eyebrow aimed at me.

I finally manage to free myself from the curtain

"Someone," I start, hooking my thumb toward Grace whose face has gone pale again. "Came home wasted. I had to give her my special hangover cure and tuck her ass into bed. Side note..." I give both Lucy and Emmett my death glare. "You two suck at taking care of the drunk birthday girl. Had I known, I would've come out so at least one of us made sure she didn't end up dead in an alley."

Lucy hangs her head in shame and hops over the curtain to jump into bed with Grace. "If it wasn't your birthday weekend, I would seriously murder you. Killer has a point. You could have died. Or been abducted. Or fell down a manhole." She throws her arms around Grace, who stifles a giggle. "But I still love you."

She pulls back and gives Grace a little shake. "But don't you ever do that to us again!"

Grace blushes apologetically. "Sorry. I...didn't want to disturb you guys."

"You'd never disturb us," Lucy says, hugging Grace tightly. "You're my best friend!"

"Okay, now that you two have had your cheesy fest, I'd like to get to bed sometime tonight. I have to be up at the crack of dawn again, like in four hours, to do my shift at the ag center before practice and class." I give them a pointed look, but they veer off on a tangent.

Lucy, who is literally petting Grace's hair, stroking it while Grace leans her head on her shoulder, starts in. "You totally missed it, though. Remember that guy you were talking to in the bar, the one with the green shirt?"

Grace nods.

"Well, after you left, he started dancing with Kailyn from your psych class. And then the next thing we knew, they were playing tonsil hockey and getting all handsy in front of everyone. Eww...so gross."

"Please tell me she did not hook up with him?" Grace asks.

"Ahem...seriously?" I interject, holding my hands in the

air in a show of objection as Emmett looks at me. "Did I not just say I need my sleep here?"

I know I'm being grouchy. That type of thing tends to happen when you have a raging case of blue balls.

"Whoa! When did you turn into a buzzkill?" Emmett says with raised eyebrows.

"Yeah. What's up with you, Killer? You're usually down to party any time, day or night," Lucy counters as she scoots to the end of Grace's bed and dangles her feet over the side.

Grace leans back against the headboard and eyes me suspiciously as well.

I throw my hands up with a frustrated grunt. "What's with the Spanish Inquisition here? Can't a guy just need to sleep?"

"Oooh," Lucy teases, glancing at Emmett in mock surprise. "Killer actually knows his historical events too. Maybe he does study!"

Everyone laughs at my expense. "Yeah, very funny. I take offense at your assumptions that I'm just a dumb jock."

Lucy leans over, blows me a kiss, and then makes a heart with her hands.

"That's not what we think. But you are acting differently than the Killer we've come to know. Is something wrong?"

I groan and slap my forehead. "Nothing is wrong with me. I'm just stressed about this independent research project."

I pause before deciding to spill it to my friends, cause if you can't be honest with your closest friends, then who can you be honest with? "I sort of...maybe slacked off a bit last year...fine, every year, and I need to make sure I keep my GPA up so I don't lose my football scholarship."

"Oh, the old GPA problem. I know how that goes,"

Emmett commiserates. "Why didn't you just say so? We could all understand that. Especially me, bro."

I shrug. "I don't know. I'm not over here sharing my life story on the daily."

Lucy throws her tiny arms around my waist and hugs me. "If you need help, I know a great tutor," she says with a wink before pulling back.

Emmett reaches out and drags her back against his chest. "Not a chance. You only get to tutor one football player and that's me, baby." He bites at her earlobe and she giggles.

"Geez, jealous much?" she coos sweetly.

Emmett picks her up and tosses her over his shoulder. "Later, you two. I'm in need of a private tutoring session."

"You are such a good student!" she quips and then squeals when he slaps her ass.

"But one you kind of love," he points out, walking them toward the door, but not before waggling his eyebrows.

I feel a twinge of jealousy. I love them both, but to see how connected they are...well, I wish I had that with someone myself. A woman I can have fun with, yet who is down-to-earth and has goals of her own to achieve. One that doesn't mind my long-term plans are to return to Iowa and put my degree to use when I take over my family farm one day.

I look back over at Grace, who's also watching our friends leave as we say our good nights. The door shuts and we're left alone once again. Grace glances back at me, questions swimming through her eyes. But they quickly vanish as she turns

off her light and rolls away from me.

"I'm tired. Goodnight, Killian."

"Grace..." I begin, hoping to clear up the earlier proposition still dangling between us.

"Nope. Stop right there." Her hand darts out behind her giving the universal sign for stop. "Please, can we...uh, just pretend none of that happened?"

"Yeah, sure. Of course."

Disappointment floods me for some reason as I get to work and rehang the fallen curtain, pausing before I pull it closed to separate us once again.

Ah, fuck it.

"But, Gracie?"

"Yeah," she says with a resigned sigh, her back still toward me.

"My offer still stands...if you want to accept it, just let me know. G'night."

I turn back and stare at my side of the room, listening to her rustling around in her bed and ignoring the pull I feel when I remember the almost kiss we had. Instead, I grab my computer and head downstairs in search of a space where temptation doesn't lie on the other side of a piece of The Great Divide.

I make it as far as the living room. Hendy's there, still awake, a game controller in his hand.

"Can't sleep either?" he asks, turning over his shoulder to watch me. "You wanna play?"

He raises the controller in the air and I shrug.

"Sure, but only for a few minutes. I need to work on this stupid project and head to bed," I mutter. I should have gone to bed before this, but now my head is filled with all things Grace and I know I won't be able to sleep.

"What's up with you, bruh?" Hendy asks as he logs us into one of the games we play. Not one of my favorites, because *Capital Offense* is still the best, but still a good one where I can turn off my brain.

"Just dealing with stuff."

"At least you aren't dealing with chick problems," Hendy says.

"What? Jessica dump your ass?" I ask.

He mumbles something that I can't make out, but I don't push it.

I press my lips firmly together to keep myself from laughing out loud. The fact that Hendy has any problems is humorous. Hendy is a total player. He's a good guy at heart, and more than just a womanizer.

We get into our game and for the next hour, I zone out. Eventually I crawl into bed, much later than planned, after deciding to skip my project tonight. I hardly realize I've fallen asleep until I hear the shower running.

When I open my eyes, sunshine pours in through one of the attic windows. Shit, I'm late for my shift in the ag center.

I scramble out of bed and text my professor that I'll be late. I hear the shower turn off and head to the bathroom, knocking like a good boy and smiling when Grace opens. She's wrapped in a towel, face pink and clean, another towel wrapped up on top of her head. She looks a lot better than she did for a while last night. She's got her toothbrush in one hand.

"Morning," I say, tipping my head to the side as I assess her. "How are you feeling today?"

She shrugs and speaks with the toothbrush in her mouth. "Better than I probably should."

I grab my toothbrush from the cup on the sink and we brush our teeth as I notice her stealing surreptitious glances my way. I'm not wearing a t-shirt and she's staring at my side.

"How'd you get that scar?" she asks, spitting out her toothpaste into the sink. My gaze follows where she's pointing.

"This one was from a dare." I laugh, twisting around to pull at the skin on my stomach.

"A dare?"

"Yeah, my brother Mac dared me to climb this fence at a neighboring farm. What we didn't know is that old man Richie hadn't removed some of the old barbed wire when they'd replaced the fence and it was hidden against the wood beam."

Her eyes widen. "Ouch. That must've hurt."

I nod in agreement, remembering the stitches and my mother yelling at me for getting into the mess. "How about you? You have any good scar stories?"

She smiles broadly, tugging the towel up her leg, the towel parting at the apex of her thighs. I swallow thickly.

"I once tripped over a rake and fell into a shovel. Had to get twelve stitches," she says proudly as she points to a long scar along the inside of her thigh.

I know Grace's dad owns a ranch, and she's lived there for several years, but she still comes across like a city girl. Which is why I cannot fathom her doing any actual farm work or using tools of any kind. Telling someone else what to do, more than likely.

"Let me guess? You were mucking out a stall?" I ask with a smirk.

She shoves my arm in protest. "I was. That time at least."

I rinse my mouth and dab my face with a towel. Grace

checks out my arm, pressing a warm finger against my bicep. I shiver with the contact.

"What about that one?"

I grin and wiggle my eyebrows. "Ever heard of cow tipping?"

"That's not even a real thing," she retorts with a snort.

"It totally is. And...let's just say the cow didn't like it when I did it and I had to run like hell, but fell when I jumped a fence."

"Dude, you need to stay away from fences." She laughs and I watch her put on make-up with an intense focus.

She's so beautiful. I don't think she even needs to wear any make-up with her flawless skin and long dark lashes that frame her brown eyes.

She catches my gaze and I look away.

"What can I say? I was a bored teenager in the middle of Bumfuck, Iowa. I did lots of stupid things."

She smiles at me in the mirror and the scent of her shampoo and the way it feels so natural talking like this is... well, it makes this attic feel like home.

Shit, Grace makes it feel like home.

She looks up at me and I swear all I hear is the blood rushing through my veins.

"So I was thinking..." she trails off as her cheeks turn red. "What if..."

"What if what, soda pop?"

"What if...I took you up on your offer?" she asks, the words coming out in a rush.

"What offer is that?" I tease, but inside I'm silently screaming *yes, please let me show you just how good I can make you feel!*

"You know..." she prods.

"Do I?"

I lean in close, shoulder to shoulder, and she sucks in a breath.

The way her eyes flash with understanding and then darken with sensual awareness tells me she knows I know what we're talking about. The offer to take her virginity.

She flusters and then gives my arm a gentle shove. "Hey, aren't you late for your shift? You need to go."

I cup her face in my hand and turn her to face me, running my thumb over the pulse point at her neck. She looks up at me from beneath her lashes.

"Just say the words, soda pop. I won't do anything until you ask. I won't show you exactly how I please a woman, not until you say the words. No matter how much I want to."

And with that, I turn and walk out leaving her to clutch at her towel, clenching her thighs, hopefully to alleviate the wetness between her legs.

Chapter Nine

G race

It's been a week since my stupid self drunkenly mentioned my virginity problem to Killian and the offer he so generously lobbed back over to fix said problem.

If you really want to lose your virginity, I'm happy to volunteer as tribute.

My heart still flutters every time I remember those words and his suggestion that I let him take my virginity.

And then the moment in the bathroom the next morning when he reaffirmed the proposition left me aching so bad between my legs that I had to do something about it after he left.

Since then, I've done my best to avoid him at all costs, spending as much time away from the house as possible.

Which is the reason I've been hanging out at the library more this week and have joined one of CFU's all-women computer clubs on campus. It's called WiSSDom, which stands for Women in Science and Software Development. Tonight was our second meeting and it was kind of nice getting to spend time with other nerdy computer geek girls like myself.

One girl is Miranda Silva, or Randi as she wants to be called. She's a sophomore who sat next to me at both the first and second meetings and we ended up partnering on a project to develop a new game app. Although it's just for fun and doesn't require a lot of my time, I found I needed a distraction and something to keep my thoughts directed away from my roommate.

The roommate I want to fuck.

But no matter what I try, something always brings me back to him. Even in my conversation with Randi.

"Do you live on or off campus?" she asks while we sit at one of the tables outside the student union, drinking coffee and discussing our app requirements.

"I was in the dorms last year, but this semester I live in a house just a block off campus. How about you?"

She lifts her hazel eyes from her laptop, peering at me from over the rim of her bright orange glasses. Her hair, also a bright orange with black streaks, is patterned in two intricate braids that fall over the front of her shoulders.

"I was never cool enough to do the sorority thing. I'm still in Wallingford Hall. But I did get a single room this year."

I smile. "That's lucky. When I was there, I lived in a suite with my two besties. But I wouldn't mind living alone at this point. Living with a..." I clear my throat. "Roommate can sometimes be a challenge."

Randi takes a sip of her coffee and sits back from the

table, folding her legs crisscross in her chair. "Oh yeah? Do you not get along with the girl you're rooming with?"

Oh, that's not quite the problem.

How do I explain my current situation? Not everyone agrees with my living arrangements. My mother, for example, was none too pleased to learn that my new roommate was a guy. A football player to boot. She said she'd read too many news stories about young college women who were forced into sex by athletes.

If only she knew how *not* forced I am...but how the offer Killian gave me has plagued my thoughts for weeks.

Ever since our almost kiss in my bed and the moments we shared in the bathroom, I've been looking at Killian in an entirely different way.

With a shake of my head, I clear my thoughts.

"Actually, I room with a guy." I pause and wait for her reaction, watching the realization dawn on Randi's face. Her eyebrows shoot up. "It's a complicated story, but Lucy, my best friend, moved in with her boyfriend, Emmett. And my other bestie, Kelsie, is studying abroad. At the time, there weren't any single rooms available, so my only option was to move into the giant attic with Killian."

Randi seems to put two and two together, her mouth forming an *O*.

"You live at Joel Henderson's football house with Killer Palmer?"

Is that what people call it? I mean, I guess it kind of is, since his dad owns it and we all just rent rooms from him.

"Yeah, I suppose I do."

Randi suddenly slaps her laptop shut and leans over in piqued interest, her elbows propped on the lid, coffee held in both hands.

"My cousin plays football too. Have you met him?

Matty Rodriguez. He's a sophomore, but I bet you've seen him."

I try to recall from the revolving door of football players that have been in the house this semester whether I've met a kid named Matty. It's the unofficial spot to hang out and chill if you're on the team. It's not a party house like the frats, but more like a place to hang, play video games, and watch movies because of the theater-style seating in the entertainment room on the main floor.

Randi pulls up some family photos in her phone and hands me one to look at. The guy is cute with a nice smile and dark hair.

I shake my head because I don't remember ever seeing him around.

"I don't think so. But then again, I don't normally hang out with all the guys if I can help it. I'm either in the kitchen or upstairs in my room studying, reading, or playing *Capital Offense*."

"Hey, I think that's the game Matty's into." Randi clicks her tongue and tilts her head to the side. "You two should go out. I think you'd find you have a lot in common. He's kinda shy and doesn't date much. Unless you already have a boyfriend or something."

I crinkle my nose. "Definitely no boyfriend."

Before I can tell her that I'm not really interested in being set up, she clicks out a message on her phone. It responds with a ping and she smiles triumphantly.

"Okay, cool. Matty's gonna join us in five."

"Wait, *what?*"

* * *

It's after dinner by the time I get home and I find it's relatively quiet in the house. Emmett, Hendy, and Killian are all still at the afternoon practice, which is where Matty will also be until he picks me up for our date tonight at eight.

Yeah, that's right.

Date.

Tonight.

I don't know why I said yes. I was put on the spot since he asked me point blank over coffee. Truthfully, Randi was right. We do seem to have a lot in common. Plus, he's super cute. He made me laugh and seeing how he and Randi were together, acting like goofy siblings, it made me feel like I could trust him.

That's a big thing for me and probably the reason I haven't lost my virginity yet. I'll date a guy a few times and find him either not meeting up to my ridiculously high standards or he'll do or say something stupid to turn me off.

I'm just finishing my hair and make-up when I hear loud voices from downstairs. The boys must be home from practice, which means Killian will be up in a few minutes. I rush into the bedroom, closing the curtain and quickly discard my towel. I pull on the panties and bra I laid out on my bed and then stare into my closet for something to wear. I'm pulling out my black leggings when I hear Killian clomping up the stairs like a giant ogre and I hum to myself *Fee, Fi, Fo, Fum...*

The door swings open and the sudden burst of air ruffles the curtain, blowing it back to give Killian an unobstructed, albeit brief, view of me standing practically naked.

He stops abruptly and stares. Then blinks. Then his fair and freckled skin turns a blotchy red. "Oh, sorry."

It's one of those awkward moments that seem to move

in slow motion. I turn my shoulders and cross my arms over my chest. "Move along! Nothing to see here."

Killian does as asked and clears his throat as I throw on my shirt and jean jacket before taking another look into the full-length mirror and tugging the curtain open.

"How do I look?"

His back is toward me as he sets his bags down on his unmade bed. He swivels his head to give me an appraising look. "Honestly, you looked better naked." He winks. "But you still look good." Then he whips his shirt over his head, revealing that muscular torso and broad shoulders of his, and throws the t-shirt on the floor as if it's done him harm. He plops down on the bed on his side, long hairy legs stretched out in front of him, and looks me over.

I wave him away "Thanks, I think."

He lifts his brows, tucking his hands behind his head. "You know you look good, Gracie. Don't give me that BS." He sniffs the air. "You smell good too. Are you going out?"

I turn away to avoid his perceptive gaze. "Yep. Got a date."

Killian jackknifes into a sitting position, swinging his legs over the side and his voice rises two octaves. "You do? With who?"

I want to respond with a sarcastic response like *What? Are you my dad?* But the look of sheer panic across his face stops me.

For whatever reason, he seems genuinely perplexed and concerned over this news. It's kind of sweet and endearing.

I pick at an imaginary piece of lint on my leggings. "Just a guy I met today. You might know him. Matty Rodriguez?"

And then as if he were a balloon, his body slumps and he literally deflates in front of my eyes.

"Oh. Matty. He's a decent guy." Killian jumps to his

feet and slowly steps into my personal space, stopping just an inch in front of me so I have to tip my head back to lock eyes. His tone is both protective and maybe even a bit jealous.

"But if Matty tries anything you don't want him to do, you tell me about it. Got it?"

I swallow. "Got it."

I sit down on the edge of my bed and slip my feet into my leather knee-high boots, zipping them up and reaching for my purse.

Before I know what he's doing, Killian grabs hold of my hand and flips it over. Then he places something in my open palm.

I stare down at the condom wrapper and let out a strangled sound.

"Just in case. It doesn't hurt to be prepared."

Chapter Ten

K illian

I look at the time in the corner of my computer screen. It's been seven minutes since the last time I checked.

Grace has been gone for two hours and fifty-three minutes and that's the fortieth time I've looked at the digital display. It's like the clock is going backwards and I'm losing my goddamn mind.

Running a hand over my face, I look at the curtain between our sides of the room. Why do I wish she was here? Why do I even care she's on a date?

But I know why. I know the fact that she might be deflowered tonight by Matty Rodriguez is driving me insane.

"For fuck's sake," I mutter angrily, leaning back in my desk chair to stare up at the glow in the dark stars on the ceiling left there by my teammate who graduated last year.

He was an astronomy major and now works for NASA or something.

"Yo, Killer! Get your ass down here!" Hendy shouts from the bottom of the stairs. "That new horror movie is out."

"I'm busy!" I yell back.

Busy worrying whether Grace is getting busy with that guy.

"The fuck you are. Marquise brought actual movie theater popcorn and Darrell brought good beer! Don't be a pussy!" Hendy yells again more forcefully, brooking no argument.

Marquise Young is one of our linebackers and a really cool guy. And Darrell Johnson is a defensive tackle. He's one of the funniest people I've met and is always playing hilarious pranks in the locker room.

On any other night, I'd normally be charging down the stairs at the idea of watching a good horror movie with my teammates and stuffing my face with buttery popcorn. But not tonight. Not when I'm sitting here wondering if Grace is doing okay. Whether she's having fun. Whether Matty is being a gentleman and not trying to...oh, fuck me.

"You have three seconds to get your ass down here, or we're coming up for you, bro," Marquise shouts up the stairs.

"Killer, come save me from these delinquents. For real, I need backup from someone with at least three brain cells," Darrell adds and I can't help but smile a little.

I'm weighing my options when Darrell bounds up the stairs holding a lightsaber he must have snagged from Hendy's room. "You want to come watch the movie," he says with a goofy grin.

"You are seriously warped, you know that?" I try not to laugh at him.

"Warped, but come on, my Jedi mind trick game is strong," he says with a wink.

"Your '80s movie tricks won't work on me," I state dryly.

He puts the lightsaber down and reaches behind him, pulling out a bucket of popcorn. "How about popcorn? Does popcorn work?" he asks as he stuffs a handful of it into his mouth. "This shit is good. Come on. You've been holed up here working on this stupid project for weeks. I need my fun, party-animal Killer back."

"Fine! But I get an entire bucket to myself and when we run drills on Monday, you make me look good."

Darrell laughs. "I mean, I'll try. We can't all just look naturally awesome all the time."

He smirks. "Oh, wait, I can." He takes off back down the stairs two at a time and I sprint after him.

I manage to tackle him to the ground as he tosses the bucket at Hendy, who somehow manages not to spill much of it.

"Fuck, bro, this floor is hard," Darrell cries out as he manages to get out from under my hold.

I laugh. "Awww...does the little baby DJ need a binkie?"

Darrell grabs a beer off the side table and chucks it at my head, but I manage to catch it.

"Will you two fuckheads knock it off? I passed on a night with Cate Donovan to hang out with you shitheads, so sit and drink the damn beer. I'm starting this movie," Hendy says as he glares at us.

"Dude, you literally just told me ten minutes ago you were going to have a booty call with Cate later after the movie," Marquise contradicts from the recliner.

"Hendy needs to get laid. Don't worry, if it's not tonight, I hear Cate is going to be at the party after the game next weekend," Darrell says jovially, slapping Hendy on the back before claiming a seat on the sofa. I take a spot in the other recliner chair.

"Where's EJ and Lucy tonight?" Darrell asks. "And your roommate? Gracie?"

At the sound of Grace's name being spoken from Darrell's mouth, I grow tense.

Hendy answers with popcorn in his mouth. "They're over at his grandmother's house. And Grace I think is on a date with Matty Rodriguez."

There's a chorus of *oohs* and *aahs* from the peanut gallery and Darrell whistles.

"How come you're not tapping that, bro?" he asks me before taking a long pull from his beer. "You gonna let that youngster Matty have all the fun with that yummy piece of—"

I'm saved from having to punch Darrell in his face with my fist when the door opens and we all startle for a moment as Grace appears in the doorway.

She looks...not very happy?

I'm now both worried about her and also somewhat pleased that there's a chance her date with Matty didn't go well. "Hey, how was the date?" I whisper over the opening credits of the movie as she stops by my chair.

She shrugs. "It was all right. Whatcha guys watching?" she asks, appearing interested in the movie.

"The new Jordan Peele horror movie with Megan Fox and Winona Ryder."

"Oh yeah, I've been waiting to see this one. Did you just start it?" She sits down on the armrest of my chair.

Hendy lets out an exaggerated groan. "Gracie, use that

giant brain of yours. Don't you see the opening credits are literally rolling right now?"

"Oh, uh, right." She chuckles, looking around the room, possibly for a place to sit. The only spot left is a small sliver of space on the couch between Darrell and Hendy. There is no way I want her near Darrell, now that I know how he feels about her.

I pull the ottoman closer to my chair, stretch out my legs and pat the leather between them. "Have a seat, soda pop."

She hesitates for a brief second and then takes the seat between my outstretched legs. Everyone grows silent as the movie begins, the scary soundtrack playing in the background, hopefully loud enough to drown out the beating of my heart.

My hands itch to touch Grace, mere centimeters away from me. To keep my hands distracted, I reach for the popcorn. I pick up the bucket from the table next to me, plunging my hand in and filling my mouth, hoping that if I keep myself occupied, I won't think about how Grace feels against me.

She turns and gives grabby hands when she sees the giant bucket. She scoots back so her butt is lodged between my legs as she reaches into the bucket and pulls out a handful of popcorn.

"Heads up, Grace," Hendy says as he tosses her a can of beer. I reach in front of her and snag it out of the air, then open it and hand it to her.

"Thank you."

She takes a few sips and hands it back to me. I turn and place it on the table. A few minutes later, I notice her rubbing a hand behind her neck. I tentatively place my hand on her shoulder to get her attention.

"You okay? Neck bothering you?" I whisper, using my

fingers to massage into the base of her neck. "Damn, your shoulders are tight."

She turns to look behind at me, and for a brief moment, I think she's going to turn me down. But then she nods and turns back to face the television, leaving me staring at the nape of her neck.

I begin to work on her shoulder muscles, massaging them gently. She makes an almost imperceptible moan as I ease a knot out of her trapezius muscle. It's not long before I feel her completely relax against me, leaning her head on my chest. Her ass settles between my thighs and there's no way she doesn't feel the growing erection that I couldn't stop even if I wanted to.

She wiggles her butt, shifting back as if to find a better position. My cock strains against my sweatpants, hoping for more of the friction.

Wait. Did she do that on purpose?

I try ignoring it and drop my hands to the sides of the armchair. She reaches for a blanket of Lucy's, tugging it over our legs like she's cold and wants the warmth.

But having felt the heat from her body, I know for a fact she is not the least bit chilly. But when her hands encircle my wrists and she lifts my arms to position them around her, I know something is going on.

"Cold?" I ask quietly, running my fingers over the skin of her forearm. Goosebumps break out over her flesh.

She nods and I squeeze my arms more tightly around her middle, my forearms grazing the underside of her breasts. Those firm, perfect breasts I've had flashes of in the bathroom. Grace squirms against me again and I stifle my desire to toss her over my shoulder and carry her upstairs.

I grab the popcorn to distract myself and offer her some.

She nods, but instead of taking some, she swivels her head and opens her mouth like a baby bird waiting to be fed.

"Seriously?" I cock an eyebrow. Is she flirting with me? Intentionally trying to entice me with these sexy moves?

Because, goddamn it, it's working. I'm so hard right now, my brain has turned to mush.

"What? I'm cozy right now."

This movie night, without a doubt, is going to kill me to get through if she keeps this up. I hold my breath and place a few pieces in her mouth, watching longingly as her lips close around my fingers. She sucks until the buttery salt is gone. And I have to use every ounce of my willpower not to come right here in my freaking sweatpants.

Grace may be a virgin, but she sure as fuck knows how to tease a man.

I'm torn between wanting to take control of this secret foreplay we have going on and letting Grace have the power to play this game of sexual tension.

I take a big inhale as she tucks her knees up under her chin and leans back against me like that for the next hour. Every move she makes, every breath she releases, reignites my need to take her upstairs and make good on the promise I made to her.

God, I want so badly for her to ask me to be the one. To be the one to take her virginity and give her something to remember forever.

It's not just her appearance. Yes, she's beautiful, but she's also insanely smart and funny. Grace Ford is the perfect woman.

The movie can't end fast enough and the minute it does, I engage in exactly sixty seconds of small talk before I make my excuses and call it a night to rush back upstairs with Grace a few steps behind me.

When we reach our room, I shut the door, panting in what sounds like I just ran a hundred-mile race.

I feel like a caged lion ready to pounce. So I fling open the curtain and stand on the far edge of the room as Grace sits down on her bed and crosses her legs in front of her, looking at me expectantly.

"So what happened on your date?" I want to watch her expression and make sure she's telling me the truth.

She grimaces. "Matty tried to kiss me."

My jaw clenches tight and my hands ball into fists. Part of me isn't sure if I can handle hearing the details of her date with my teammate. The other part wants desperately to find out.

But before I can ask her to expound, she continues. "I didn't want to kiss him back."

I frown, confused by her statement. "Why not?"

She swivels on her bed, throws her legs over the side, and walks over to where I stand. She lays a hand over my chest and raises on tip-toe until her eyes are at my chin level. I go still, waiting for what she has to say.

"Because, Killian. I wanted it to be you."

Chapter Eleven

G race

I think I've stunned him stupid because Killian's only movement is to blink.

Once.

Twice.

He stares at me, his mouth twisting in confusion and his brows furrow inward. I lift up on my tip-toes and cup his face in my hands, tipping his head back slightly before I kiss him. It's soft and tentative at first. Just a peck, but enough to show him that I mean this. I'm serious about where this goes next.

"I've dreamt about this," I whisper, kissing his forehead, then his jaw, then his ear before trailing my lips down his corded neck. My fingers dig into his soft wavy hair. I breathe in his intoxicating spicy scent.

"About what?"

I pull back just enough to stare into his darkened eyes. They look at me with longing and lust.

My fingers lace behind his head and I walk him back to the edge of his bed, pushing him down before I swing my leg over his thigh, fitting myself on top of his lap. I can feel the hard ridge of his cock now fitting snugly against the wet crotch of my panties. They've been wet since he started touching me downstairs.

Holy shit, I've never been so turned on by a guy's hands on my shoulders before.

Which was why I had a whole internal argument with myself over this decision. While everyone else watched the movie, I debated the merits of sleeping with Killian.

We're supposed to be friends. Just roommates. But this is going to change us.

We'll be lovers now. Even if it happens just this one time.

Killian Palmer will always be my first.

"All I've thought about since my birthday is what it would be like to kiss you. To have you on top of me. To feel you inside me."

Our lips crash with fiery purpose. Our kiss is incendiary and it's as if our bodies confess that we no longer want to be just friends.

A growl reverberates from somewhere deep within Killian's chest and he swings an arm around my waist and tackles me against the mattress.

Making a breathy sound, I let out a puff of air. Killian is so huge and could crush me with his body weight. Yet, he doesn't. There's something almost gentle about the way he holds himself above me, hovering his weight above me.

"I've wanted that too." He kisses my nose and then my cheek. I feel him everywhere, but especially his erection between my legs. God, he's so big. His mouth covers mine when he adds, "I've wanted this for so long."

My stomach flutters with unrestrained excitement and nerves.

"Will you go slow with me? Because, you know... I'm a..."

Killian sits back, tugging the neck of his shirt and pulling it over his head to expose his perfectly sculpted chest. He smiles as he takes my hand and places it between his pecs. His chest is so solid, with tufts of golden-red hair in the center that I brush my fingertips over. I feel the fast *thump-thump-thump* of his heartbeat as I spread my fingers, my pinky grazing the outer rim of his circular nipple. He rolls our joined hands slowly over his chest.

"I know, Grace. I'll go as slow or as fast as you want. And I promise to make you feel good."

Every muscle in my body tenses with anticipation and with the thrill of knowing Killian will make me feel good. I trust him to come through on his promise.

For having such large hands, he's surprisingly deft at unbuttoning my shirt and removing it with ease, leaving me in the tank top I wore underneath. He cups both breasts in his hands and a low groan escapes his throat as his thumbs circle over the soft fabric covering my puckered nipples.

I close my eyes as the erotic sensation rips through my body going straight to my clit. I clench my thighs together looking to ease the physical commotion stirring in my body.

"Can I kiss you here?" Killian asks, plumping the flesh of my boobs.

I feel the blush form and fan over my chest.

"You don't have to ask...but yes. Please."

His attention moves to my breasts, pulling the straps of the tank and my bra over my shoulders to expose my boobs.

He makes a noise—a cross between a groan and a sigh of relief—and then his mouth is on me. His wet tongue flicks over the sensitive peak of one nipple and then the other as his fingers continue to toy with each breast. The achy need between my legs ratchets up to a level I've never felt before. It throbs with an incessant desire to be filled. My hips arch up to meet his crotch and I hear Killian chuckle.

"Impatient, are we?"

I lift my head to look down at him.

"I want to get to the good part," I retort.

Without missing a beat, Killian props his hands next to my shoulders and rolls his hips over mine, the sensation so igniting I think I've just burst into flames.

"You mean this part?"

He aligns his steely cock in the center of my pelvis and glides it over my clit. I nearly convulse with pleasure.

"Oh, God. Yes, that part." I grab both of his ass cheeks and squeeze. He still has his jeans on and I'm in my leggings, which are far too many clothes for my liking. I wiggle underneath him. "I want to get you naked."

As if I just pushed on the launch button, Killian pops up and salutes me. "Yes, ma'am. Me and the Killer D are at your service."

He begins to unbutton his jeans when I snort in laughter. "Killer D?"

Killian smirks, waggling his eyebrows, pointing down to his erection that I can see now poking through the top of his briefs.

"Yeah, you know. The killer dick in my pants."

"Oh, my God, you're such a dork!" I laugh, but then stop, my eyes widening when I finally get a good look at what Killian has been hiding in his pants all this time.

I mean, sure, I've seen the outline under his towel and

those freaking sexy sweats he wears around the house, so I knew he was packing.

But guys have a tendency to exaggerate wildly when they talk about their dicks. I live in a house full of cocky jocks who go on and on about the size of their units all the damn time.

But having the up-close-and-personal vantage point I have right now is eye opening, to say the least.

The Killer D is not just a fabricated concoction of a tall tale said to impress his friends.

He. Is. Huge.

I swallow thickly, suddenly becoming a little worried about what comes next.

Killian takes my hand and fits it around his erection, the silky heat of him pulling me out of my enthralled shock. I blink up at him. My fingers barely reach around his shaft. He winks and wears the sexiest grin I've ever seen on him.

"The Killer D doesn't bite. I promise, soda pop."

His usual over-the-top remark reminds me of who I'm with and I smirk back.

"But *I* might."

His laughter stops as I begin stroking him in earnest, circling the crown and running my fingernail over the tip. Pre-cum pools at the head and I swirl it around, fascinated more by the sexy groan that escapes his chest that matches that smile.

"That feels fucking good. Grip me tighter."

I do as he asks, happy with the praise and direction he gives.

One of the things I like the most about Killian is he is really good at speaking his mind. He doesn't hold things back with me or his friends. I've also heard him on the phone talking with his brothers and I hear him giving great advice and sharing his thoughts on things they are dealing with.

Killian Palmer is a really good guy.

Maybe that's the thing I find sexiest about Killian. He's just a good person, and I trust him to be gentle with me and give me what I need tonight.

"Um, Grace," he pants, pushing my hand away after a few seconds. "If we want to get to that other good part, I'm gonna need you to stop."

"Oh, sorry." I grin sheepishly, not realizing how easy it would be to get him so quickly turned on and ready to go over the edge.

My thoughts vanish in a flash when suddenly he's hooked his thumbs in the top of my leggings and he divests me of them and my panties.

I've never been overly concerned about my physical attributes. I've always been on the thin side, but that doesn't mean I have a perfect body by any means. But the weight of Killian's unabashed concentration on my now naked body makes me feel a little self-conscious.

"You're a goddamn wet dream," he murmurs, maybe more to himself than to me. But then, with a rasp in his voice, he says, "I am going to devour you."

Devour? Is that a good thing? Because I've seen him stick a whole pizza in his mouth. He is not graceful.

But in this context, maybe his statement has merit.

Killian disappears down the bed as he slides his lips across my belly and all I can see now is the top of his head and his broad shoulders.

The first contact of his tongue as he circles my belly button is enough sensation that I buck my hips skyward.

"Whoa there, cowgirl. I'm not even close to the main

attraction yet." He chuckles with his lips pressed against my contracting ab muscles.

Placing wet kisses along my flesh, he moves south until he's dead center between my legs. Killian swipes between my folds, dropping more kisses against the insides of my thighs. He captures both legs in his strong grip and spreads me wider.

I experience a slew of anxiousness that hits me all at once as he drags his tongue through my bare sex. I drop my hand to the top of his head, ready to push him away and stop this madness when he breathes me in deeply and sucks my clit between his lips. Oh, holy mother....

I pant and we both moan out in sync.

And then his finger drags through my wet center and, with a quick motion, a large finger thrusts inside. I let out a gasp of surprise that quickly turns to pleasure when his finger moves inside me.

"Killian," I say, uncertain of whether I want him to stop or keep going. He adds another finger and his tongue swirls over my clit. I whimper, muttering incoherently. "Don't stop."

He continues pumping his fingers in a timely and rhythmic dance until my body is seizing up with pleasure. I begin to feel that euphoria wash over me until I'm dancing on clouds and speaking in tongues.

When I finally come down from my orgasm, Killian has moved up to my side, gently caressing a hand along my sides and belly until he kisses me deeply. I taste myself on his tongue and I sigh, rolling to my side to face him, stroking my hand down his chest, the coarse hairs tickling my fingers, until I wrap my leg over his hip and my hand around his dick.

I buck my hips and bring the tip of his cock to my entrance that's wet and achy for him.

He jerks away. "Fuck, Grace. Let me get a condom first."

I lock my leg tighter, hooking my heel into the small of his back and rolling him on top of me so that his length is lined up perfectly with my pussy.

"I'm on birth control." I make my case for what I want and that's him bare. "You're my first Killian. I want to feel all of you."

Killian's head drops forward, his soft hair brushing under my nose. His face is buried in my pillow at my ear and he's breathing hard.

"Fuck, Grace. Are you trying to kill me?"

I thread my fingers through his hair and yank his head up so I can kiss him.

"Wouldn't be the worst way to go, would it?"

I spread my legs wider, feeling the tip of his dick sliding through my wetness. He hisses.

"At least if I die, I'll be in heaven."

Chapter Twelve

K illian

Bracing my arms on either side of Grace's head, I slide my dick through her wetness until I feel it nudge at her entrance.

"I don't want to hurt you, soda pop," I whisper as I look into her eyes that gaze back at me with a mixture of fear and desire.

"You won't," she promises, urging me with a buck of her hips. But I know that no matter how slow I take this, there's going to be a moment or two of discomfort for her.

I ease the tip of my erection further inside, feeling her warmth surround me and then pull back slowly, sliding in inch by inch with each gentle thrust. She grabs my hips with her fingers, nails biting into my flesh, and her legs clench me tight.

"Relax," I say. "Let me take my time."

It's killing me to go this slow. She's so incredibly wet and tight I have to use every ounce of control I have to keep my cock from ramming into her virgin territory. My body trembles with need, but the trusting gaze on Grace's face grounds me and keeps me from losing myself in the heat squeezing my cock.

When I manage to push halfway to my hilt, she grimaces in pain and her muscles clamp down around me.

"Fuck, Grace," I manage to groan, lifting one hand to caress her jaw. "I'm sorry this hurts."

"Killer D's nickname is...completely on brand," she says with a wry chuckle, her jaw clenched and her eyes squeezed shut.

"I'm trying so hard to be gentle with you," I reply, sliding out to the tip. Her muscles relax again and I go back to the excruciatingly slow movement. "Just tell me if I need to stop."

I decide I need another tactic. Bracing myself up with a palm on the mattress, I lower my hand and reach between us, finding her clit, swirling my thumb around the sensitive and swollen nub.

"Oh, my God, Killian. Please don't stop!"

I keep circling her clit as I manage to push deeper into her tight channel. I've been through this once before with a high school girlfriend. Only then, I didn't realize Killer D could cause pain, so I really botched that experience. I felt horrible about it.

Eventually, I got better, listening and learning how to get a woman ready for sex before I even attempted full-on penetration.

And because Grace is so small, I have to pull out all the stops to get her there. I'm still only three-quarters of the way inside her now, but I need to go further until I'm buried so deep there's no more space between us. I stare down to where we're joined, enjoying the view of my cock sliding in and out of her.

"You have no idea how hot it is to watch your body taking me in," I groan, my gaze finding hers again as she looks at me with wonder and amazement.

"I don't know if I can take any more of your Killer D, though," she says as she bites her lower lip.

"I have an idea." I put my weight on my knees and reach next to her head to grab a second pillow. Slipping my hand underneath her hips, I lift her up enough to slide the pillow under her ass, tilting her toward me. Then I grip behind her calves, pressing against her legs as I cautiously lean forward. Her ankles come to rest on the tops of my shoulders and I slowly sink into her until I bottom out with a long groan.

"Fuuuuck..."

She gasps. "Oh, my God! You're so deep."

I don't move for a second as I give her time to acclimate and me time to pull it together so I don't come in five seconds. I let out a deep, shaky breath.

"You okay?" I ask, searching her lidded eyes for her response.

She nods.

"Words, Grace. Give me the words."

"I'm fine now, I think. You can move," she urges as she squirms beneath me. She has no idea how good that feels. "I'm okay now."

"Here, grab the headboard," I suggest, and I place her hands on the slats in the headboard behind her head. Her small fingers clasp it in her grip and I finally start to move, my pulse quickening with every thrust. Each time I bury myself and graze her clit, she gasps and moans. Her hands fly out and reach for me. Her fingernails dig into my backside and I thrust harder.

"Yes, just like that," Grace sighs, her mouth opening in pleasure.

I close my eyes and focus on feeling her body around me. She's a perfect fit. I feel every inch of her as I glide in and out, over and over again. My arms are braced on either side of her, my hips pistoning as I rub my pelvis against hers. I change the rhythm of my movements to short and deep pulses, positioning against her clit with my pelvic bone.

She moans and squirms beneath me, seeking more friction. I grin against her jaw. Grace clearly likes her clit played with while I'm inside her, so I reach between us again and circle her clit with my thumb.

"Yes!" she cries out as her body begins to tremble, her head thrashing against the pillow.

"That's it, Grace. I want to feel you come," I encourage softly, panting as I continue my movements, keeping my pace as steady as I can.

Her lips part and on a silent cry, her hips undulate, her muscles spasming around my cock, taking me over the edge with one final push.

"Oh fuck, yes!" I bellow, slamming into her. I lose control as my balls tighten and I'm coming hard, my release gushing inside her body. I give one final pump and my body relaxes, my cock still nestled deep inside. I feel her pussy give me a final aftershock squeeze.

I want to stay here forever, inside her warm chamber, and never leave. I let my weight rest on my knees and arms so I don't crush her and turn my face into her hair, kissing the side of her head.

"Wow," she whispers.

I slowly move, lifting her ankles from over my shoulders and placing her legs on the bed.

I stare down at our joined bodies as I pull out. Something about seeing my release spilling from her makes me feel like a possessive caveman. Like I've just branded her as mine forever. And maybe, in some way, I have.

I'll always be her first.

I'm overcome with the need to mark her, and gently run my thumb through the slickness between her legs and succumb to the desire. She stares down at her belly, where I paint a small swath of cum across the soft flesh of her abdomen. Grace sucks in a breath, her eyes blazing with sensuality, and she drags her own fingertip through it, tracing it in a circle.

Hottest thing ever.

But then I come back to reality as the blood returns to my brain and I remember this was her first time.

"Are you okay, Grace?" I ask, my eyes finding hers. "Did I hurt you?"

A smile of contentment tips at the corners of her mouth and a faint blush pinks her neck and cheeks.

"I think I'm better than okay. That was so good."

Grinning proudly, I bask in the feel of her praise.

But then she shakes her head. "I'm definitely going to feel it tomorrow, but it was sooo worth it."

Then she turns away and bites her lip.

"What is it?" I ask, rolling to my side and slipping my arm underneath her head. I press my fingertips into her chin and turn her back to face me.

"I just didn't think it would be like that the first time," she admits, her blush intensifying. "I mean, it was a little uncomfortable at first, but then..."

She trails off, but looks at me in complete awe and I feel like a goddamn superhero.

Leaning down, I plant a soft kiss on the tip of her nose. "What can I say, soda pop? Now you know why it's called the Killer D," I tease. "And he was happy to be of assistance. Feel free to use him anytime you like."

She stiffens slightly and I pull back to search her dark eyes. Did I say something wrong? I was feeling so fucking close to her just now and not just physically.

Almost like this was meant to be and I can feel myself falling for my roommate. Suddenly, I realize I need to stop this line of thinking. Grace asked me to help rid her of her virginity, but she didn't say she wanted a relationship.

No matter how badly I might want to see where this goes with her, I need to respect her wishes.

Grace moves gingerly to the side of the bed, searching for a shirt. I lean down and hand her my t-shirt.

"I need to get cleaned up," She says shyly, turning her back to me as she slides the oversized shirt over her small frame.

I sit up and throw my legs over the side of the bed, completely unconcerned that I'm naked or that my softening cock is hanging limply now between my legs. After what we did together, there should be no more barriers between us.

"Come here," I demand, opening my arms to her. She cocks her head to the side and I wiggle my fingers for her to step inside my spread legs. She's just a head taller than me like this, and it puts her tits just at the right height. I lean in, shuck up the shirt and suck a nipple between my lips.

"OMG! Stop it... you are such a boy!" She laughs, trying to squirm away, but then moans when I wrap my arm around her waist, tugging her tight and flick my tongue over her sensitive peak. I release her before I let myself get hard again. There's no way she can take me again this soon after her first time.

"Let's go shower," I say, standing up and hoisting her up on my back. She wraps her arms and legs around me and rests her chin on my shoulder as I carry her to our shared bathroom. Grace pulls the t-shirt she's wearing overhead, while still clinging to my back. I watch in the mirror as it falls to the ground. Our eyes meet in the reflection and we stare for a long moment, unspoken words seeming to pass between us.

After a beat, I turn on the shower faucet and once the water turns warm, I step inside, turning so Grace gets the spray on her back. She slowly releases her grip and slides down my body. Reaching for the bar of soap, I begin lathering it up in my hands, then move them over her body, caressing her stomach and between her legs. She presses a palm against the wet tile and tips her head back, enjoying the sensation. The move pushes her chest out and I lather her tits in my hands, working the suds up nice and frothy.

"Who knew the giant could be so gentle?" she says, lifting her head and reaching for the bar of soap.

I shrug. "I have my moments."

Her hands immediately land on my stomach, gliding over my abdominals. My cock twitches in hopes she'll go lower.

"How are you real?" she asks on a reflective sigh, tracing each muscle with a finger.

I laugh. "What do you mean—real?"

"I mean...you are physically perfect. You're smart. You're funny." She glances up at me under thick lashes and moves her hand south, making me suck in a breath when her soapy fingers roam over my dick and balls. As if knowing I'll not withstand that line of torture, she quickly moves back to my abs.

"I'm real, soda pop. And I'm far from perfect. I have a few flaws."

She steps aside to let me rinse and laughs. "Very true. Like your penchant for untidiness."

"Don't knock my visually appealing organization system," I joke, turning the water off once we're both clean.

She steps out of the shower and hands me my towel. "Visually appealing? I would believe it if you said you were born in a barn."

Laughing at her close assessment, I toss my wet towel back on the hook and we walk back into our room...our shared bedroom. The one we just had sex in and now have to figure out the protocol for the after-sex situation.

If she were any other girl, I wouldn't have her stay the night or cuddle. But this is her room too. I'm not sure how she wants to play this.

I stop by the end of her bed and wait for her to call the shots.

"I'm not normally a cuddler," I state, trying to make this situation less awkward for her. "But if you want, we can..."

I swear I see a flicker of hurt on her face and I hate that I said that, but it's too late to retract my statement. Her body is swallowed in my large t-shirt and all I want to do is take it off and hold her in my arms all night long.

She walks over to her bed and pats the empty side of it.

"Just come lie down for a minute. You can sleep in your bed. I just...let's not make this weird, okay?" she says, looking at me with hopeful eyes.

Is that hope that we can remain friends? Or hope that this could be more?

Shit. I'm probably reading too much into it. I decide to

follow her lead tonight and do what she asks. After all, her first time is one of those core memory moments for her.

"You got it," I agree, sitting up against her headboard as she nestles under the crook of my arm, burrowing in like a small bunny. "But I can't promise the Killer D won't get hard again. He doesn't understand snuggling."

Grace laughs and lays a small hand on my chest. It's soft and warm, just like her.

"Well then, let's distract him. Tell me about your family's farm."

Apropos of nothing, her question does the trick and diverts the conversation away from what just happened between us, clearly avoiding that topic entirely.

I begin to tell her stories of the farm and my brothers until I feel her soft breaths slow against my chest. When I look down fifteen minutes later, I find her fast asleep.

I place a soft kiss to the top of her head, breathing in the scent of her shampoo and whisper into her hair.

"I think I'm falling in love with you, Grace."

Chapter Thirteen

G race

The fall breeze tickles my nose as I walk along the tree-lined road the two blocks to campus. Gold, red, and copper leaves line the sidewalk, the scent of autumn wafting through the air, the sun warming my face and skin as I look up to the cloudless sky.

I smile from the contented feeling that swirls through my bloodstream, sending tingles up and down my spine and right into my belly. And elsewhere.

When I woke this morning, I knew Killian was already gone, having left early for the agricultural center before his football practice. But when I rolled over, I could still smell him on my pillow and I clutched it to my face, grinning like an idiot.

My mind keeps retracing every single moment of last night like a finger-painting, etched in my memories forever.

I gave my virginity to Killian.

My friend. My roommate.

And now my...lover?

I tug at my backpack strap with both hands, now slightly uncomfortable and nervous about what things will be like between us the next time we see each other, which will likely be later tonight.

We agreed this wouldn't need to change our relationship. I told him in no uncertain terms that I'm not looking for a boyfriend. Or even a regular hookup. In my mind, this was a one-and-done.

Killian seemed to be in agreement. But even so, and if the odds are good that we remain friends, how will I ever unsee his naked body writhing on top of me? I'm always going to think of the Killer D in his pants and blush. Lord help me.

And then there's the way he was so deliberately tender and gentle with me. I can still feel the tight ripples of his corded muscles and glutes against my fingers as I rolled my hands up and down his back. I remember the heat of his body and how his hard erection felt when he buried himself inside me.

Just the memory of his cock filling me has my inner walls clenching and my tummy fluttering like a piece of me is empty and has gone missing.

Sheesh, I didn't realize having sex with Killian would turn me into some sex-starved addict wanting it again so soon. I'm craving it like a vampire needing to feed.

It was only last year when I teased Lucy about how she was always so desperate for Emmett's dick and how she seemed addicted to sex. I joked at how she'd become a horny woman. But now I understand the nagging need to satiate the hunger for sex. It's not as humorous a predicament as I once thought.

Because now I crave sex.

I couldn't even take a damn shower without the memory of how his cock felt in my hand when I lathered him up. I had to turn on the cold water to full blast this morning just to douse the growing ache between my legs.

Maybe a friends-with-benefits arrangement wouldn't be such a bad idea. Kelsie had something like that our freshman year with a senior from one of the frats. They each got what they needed, had fun booty calls, and never got serious.

As I enter the student union for a coffee pit stop before heading to my computer science lab, I make a mental note to ask Killian about it this weekend. Opening the door, a rush of cool air slaps me out of my thoughts, and my eyes adjust to the lower level of light. I immediately hear Killian's voice before I see him. Scanning the cafe tables in the center of the atrium, I see him talking to a few football players, seemingly regaling them with what must be a crazy story about Lord knows what because they are all laughing hysterically.

That's Killian for you. He knows how to make people laugh. He's always doing things to make me laugh too.

My belly flutters with a strange feeling that I can't quite pinpoint.

I see him out of the corner of my eye, but don't want to gain his attention, so I creep behind him as covertly as possible en route to the coffee bar. As if he has radar, he turns suddenly, stops talking mid sentence, and our eyes connect. A sizzle and zap flares down my spine just as sure as if I touched a live wire.

"Hey, soda pop," he says, his smile bright and welcoming. But the look he gives me is more carnal than I've ever seen him give me before. I clench my thighs together to stave off that ever-present tingle and try to sound unaffected in return.

I give him a wave. "Hey, roomie."

He jumps to his feet and grabs his bag, hooking it over his shoulder and turning his head to speak over his shoulder to his friends. "I'll catch you guys later."

Killian sidles up next to me in line, his fresh, clean scent mixed with a spicy cologne giving me strange urges I've never felt until now.

Like an urge to climb him like a tree and yell, "You Tarzan. Me Jane. Take me home and make wild love with me."

I swallow down my bizarre imagery and step in line behind a girl with curly red hair that reminds me of a Strawberry Shortcake doll. I ignore the way the heat of his arm feels when it casually brushes against mine.

"Whatcha in the mood for?" he asks curiously.

My head snaps up to look at him, wondering if he can read my very dirty thoughts right now. Whatever he sees in my expression has him cocking a knowing brow. I feel my cheeks heat with embarrassment from being caught in my inappropriate thoughts, and I quickly look down at my feet, mumbling my response.

"Just a coffee."

Not sex.

He bumps me with his shoulder and chuckles. "Gee, Captain Obvious. I'd never guess you were here to get coffee at 8:00 a.m."

Then his voice goes low and deep and it sends prickles of desire straight down to my center. "Did the Killer D keep you awake all night?"

I snort lamely, ready to make a sarcastic remark, but instead just agree with him. "Yeah, my roommate is so inconsiderate that way."

His fingers find my ribs and he tickles me as I squirm and hiss loudly, garnering the attention of both the barista and Strawberry Shortcake girl.

"Stop it!" I laugh, pushing his hands away and wiggling out of his hold. He finally does and I give him an inquisitive look. "What are you doing here, by the way? Thought you had practice this morning."

Killian drapes an arm around my neck in a casual manner, the gesture feeling both friendly yet kind of romantically sweet too. I breathe in a huge dose of him and allow this momentary sense of relaxation.

"I did have practice and I have some time before I need to be out at the ag center again to check on Mama Frieda. She's about ready to pop out her baby calf. Figured I'd grab some brekky and coffee because things are about to go down." He accentuates the last word with a long *awwwwwon* and it makes me laugh.

"You're a weirdo. Who else but you would get this excited about the birth of a cow?"

I step up to the counter to place my usual order while Killian gapes at me as if I've just mentioned I smothered my grandmother in her sleep.

"I'll take a venti skim mocha latte," I say when the barista asks me what I want. Then I look longingly at the bakery selection. "And one of the cinnamon rolls, please."

She punches in the computer keypad. "That'll be $8.50, please."

I open my wallet to extract a ten-dollar bill, but Killian beats me to the punch, handing over what looks like a loyalty card.

"Here, just take it from this."

I push his arm away in objection, but he's too fast and strong so it's no use.

I'm uncertain whether this is just his way of being friendly, so to speak, or if it means something else. Like his buying me breakfast because we did the down-and-dirty. I don't want this to get awkward between us.

We move to the end of the counter to wait for my coffee and Killian gives me a questioning look, his head tipping to the side as if trying to figure me out.

"How can you not get excited about a new baby calf, Gracie? Weren't you raised on a ranch?"

I roll my eyes. "Yeah, sort of. But ranching is my dad's thing. I could live without it. Usually when I'm at home, I hang in the house, read, or play video games."

Killian gives me an odd look and then chuckles. "I'm surprised. You don't seem like a gamer."

The barista sets down my hot coffee and warm cinnamon roll on the counter in front of us. Killian reaches for the pastry, grabs two forks from the dispenser, and I pick up my coffee.

He leads me to an empty table and we take seats next to each other.

"Do you honestly think I'm going to share my roll with you?" I say with a lift of my eyebrow to which he just smirks, picks up the fork, and digs into the gooey pastry. Then he brings it toward my mouth and I open expectantly, waiting to take the first bite.

But before I can wrap my lips around it, the roll disappears and he shoves it in his open mouth with a groan.

I gouge him in the ribs with my elbow "Rude, much?"

Killian lets out a boisterous laugh and then offers me

another bite. I lean in toward the fork, eying him suspiciously until I take the bite.

We devour the cinnamon roll in less than three seconds flat.

And I'm not sure which is sweeter.

The taste of the cinnamon goodness on my tongue or the unexpected kiss and words Killian leaves me with before he heads off to his next stop.

"That tastes good." He leans in close and his lips brush mine. "But not nearly as good as you, Grace."

And then he disappears and my heart literally becomes as gooey as the icing on the pastry.

Damn him for being more than I bargained for.

Chapter Fourteen

K illian

I grin stupidly even though I'm completely stressed out at the moment.

I put my phone in my pocket, wishing I was back in Grace's bed instead of delivering a calf. Hell, I'd take a long, hard football practice over this stress.

"You got this, Mama," I coax as I rub the heifer's backside. "You're nearly there. Let's get this calf out. See, Old Bessie had hers. It's not so hard," I add as I glance over at the cow that had her calf a few days ago. I check her again and look nervously around. I need to call Professor Schmidt, along with his vet assistant, so they know what I'm dealing with right now. The calf feels like it has one leg forward instead of two. Shit.

I'm about to call my professor when I hear the side door of the large barn enclosure open and then quietly close. I assume it's Leonard, the vet assistant, and I breathe out a sigh of relief. But then I freeze when I turn and see Grace standing there looking like a beautiful apparition.

"Grace?" I quickly remove the elbow-high glove and walk over to the edge of the stall.

"Hey..." she trails off and looks at Mama Freida. "Is that your cow?"

Her eyes widen as Mama Freida moos loudly, whether in greeting or pain, I'm not sure. I turn to see a hoof sticking out, the newborn moving through the birth canal and I grimace.

"Goddamn it," I mutter, stepping back into the stall and yanking my phone out again to call my professor. He picks up on the second ring.

"Hey, Killian. Didn't expect to hear from you. How's Mama doing?" he answers cheerfully, as if I'm just calling to chit-chat. Far from it. I'm in a state of panic and emergency, uncertain of how I'll do this alone.

"Calf is abnormal anterior with one hoof forward," I state, skipping all formality and niceties.

"Well, shoot. Okay then, I'll call Leonard and get over there as soon as I can. But you might need to help her with some heavy lifting, if you know what I mean. Just like we talked about before. You got this, kid," he says before hanging up.

I stare at the phone. Is he fucking serious? I'm no veterinarian, and this isn't exactly what I signed up for. I've been here to make sure Mama was cared for with her breakfast and to clean up. Not to deliver a calf without vet assistance.

This isn't new to me, by any means, and I've seen these things before. I grew up on a farm. But we always called the local vet when things got tough.

"Killian?" Grace's voice breaks me from my anxious thoughts. I turn around to see she's just outside the stall and is putting on gloves like she's about to come in and help, but that's crazy. It's Grace we're talking about. My city girl roommate.

"What are you planning to do?" I ask, voice breaking a little like a pubescent boy.

"I'm going to help." She motions with a gloved hand toward Mama Frieda. "You both look like you need it. Plus, I've seen my dad and the vet do this once. *We* can do this together, otherwise she or her calf may not make it."

I swallow and nod, her confident conviction in this togetherness sparking something inside of me that has me wanting to salute with a shout, "Yes, ma'am!"

I slide my arm through the glove again and begin to explain what we need to do, but she seems clearly capable of performing the necessary tasks without my instruction.

"You're going to need to pull. I'm not strong enough," Grace says as she leans in a little to examine the situation.

"Actually, your arms are smaller and will probably fit better. I'll get in over you and help extract, but you go in first."

We begin to work to help get the calf delivered. It takes a few contractions and strong pulls from both of us, but several minutes later, a calf comes sailing out, knocking Grace backwards into me as we both stumble to the ground. The newborn lands on top of us, limbs weak and covered with amniotic fluid. Or as Mac calls it, birthing goo. It looks like we were on one of those Nickelodeon shows where the guests get doused with loads of slime.

Grace sits up, her shoulders stiff and back to me. I can't see her face, but for a second I think she's about to go off on how gross this all is, and how her shirt and jeans are all dirty now and I'll have to buy her a new pair of shoes.

But instead, she kneels next to the calf and, with steady hands, begins to check it out, making sure everything is accounted for as the calf struggles to stand on wobbly legs.

"Ahh, aren't you a perfect little guy," she coos to the calf, then turns to face me with a beaming smile. "We did it, Killian!"

I nod in utter disbelief. "We sure did."

I move to her side and get to work assessing the calf's breathing and his limbs, just as Professor Schmidt rushes inside and over to the stall.

"Well looky here! We have a newborn. Nice work, Killian," he says proudly, seemingly not noticing Grace by my side, who is grinning at the newborn like a fool.

I beam under his compliment, looking over to Grace as she turns her smile to me.

"I did have some help, though," I note, removing my slimy glove and motioning over to Grace. "I couldn't have done it without my amazing assistant."

Professor Schmidt's gaze follows the direction of my hand and he smiles at Grace. "And just who is my new recruit?"

"This is...Grace. My roommate," I fumble with the right word to describe her, adding roommate too quickly.

Grace removes her gloves and holds out her hand to shake the professor's as he nods his appreciation. "Any chance you'll consider a major in agricultural studies?"

She shakes her head and chuckles. "Probably not. Computers and computer programming are more my thing. I'll leave the cow fun to Killian going forward. But it was fun helping out."

She gives me a furtive glance, and her arm brushes against my forearm like she's naturally gravitated toward me.

Professor raises an eyebrow. "Well, we all know we need more women in STEM, so I'm glad you found your calling. Seems like you and Killian share a common bond. I've tried to convince him to minor in computer studies to no avail. But you are welcome back anytime with Killian."

The professor swings his head over toward the pen where Mama and baby are now resting comfortably. "I should get them both checked out now. You two can go get cleaned up and get on with the rest of your day. Thanks again for all your help."

"No problem, Professor. I'll stop over tomorrow before we leave for our road game," I add, bending down to pick up my backpack and grab Grace's hand in mine.

The professor dismisses us with a brisk wave, focusing on both mom and baby, who bellow softly as we walk hand in hand out the main barn doors.

Grace takes two quick steps to my every one, as we head outside into the cool autumn air. I suck in a lungful of the fresh air and feel a weight lift from my chest.

"Hey, what was the comment the professor made about you minoring in computer studies?" Grace asks, glancing at me curiously.

I keep walking, tugging her along, shaking my head to discount her question. "Oh, it's nothing really."

I did one thing for the department last semester and

now Professor Schmidt thinks I'm a computer genius. Which I'm not.

My computer skills pale in comparison to Grace's, I'm sure. And really I'm not that knowledgeable of all the ins and outs of programming or software development. I coded one thing to help track the birthing rates of the animals last year and now the professor wants me to delve into it as a way to augment my agricultural studies. But Grace doesn't need to know any of that. She'd probably laugh at how lame it sounds.

Her pace slows down considerably and I stop, wondering what's up. When I glance down at her, I can tell she seems hurt that I shut her out. Now I feel like a big jerk.

Hoping to move off the topic entirely, I place my hands on her shoulders and stare into her dark eyes.

"Grace, thank you for helping me out in there." I nod my head behind us toward the barn, trying to find the right words to describe what her showing up and helping me out means to me. "That was..."

A smile forms across her mouth. "Crazy fun?"

My lips twitch and I let out a breathy laugh. "Intense?"

"Definitely not a place you should ever bring a first date?"

"Or a second date either?"

She laughs and shakes her head.

"Seriously, though, you were incredible. I...I'm sorry I underestimated your farming skills," I admit with a sheepish grin.

"It's not like this city girl walks around advertising my cattle doula skills."

"Cattle doula?"

I watch her face flush. My mind immediately transports back to how her face pinked when I made her orgasm.

Would she let me do that again? Would my interest in her be too obvious if I suggested it? Maybe I can just play it cool and offer to be her fuck buddy. It certainly would be a convenient setup.

"Why are you staring at me like that, farm boy?" she asks.

Wordlessly, I glance around us, looking for a spot where we can have some privacy.

Clearing my throat, I tug her toward the grassy area between the two farm buildings. The minute we're concealed from view, I spin her around and gently press her back against the red brick wall.

I lean down and murmur, "Because I was thinking of doing this again."

I kiss her.

At first she tenses and I start to pull away, but then her hands clench my shirt, pulling me closer to her. Our kiss intensifies and I feel this connection with her. A connection deeper than I've ever felt before and it's exhilarating and scary all at the same time. Does she feel the same way? Am I overthinking this? Fuck. I don't want to fuck this up and lose her from my life.

I hear the sounds of some other ag students approaching and I step away abruptly, breaking our kiss and wishing we were somewhere private.

Like our bedroom.

"Come on, we need to get cleaned up." I offer my hand for her to take and she slides hers into it. I rub my thumb over the smooth skin on the palm of her small hand.

We walk briskly, not talking, but there's something there.

We're a...vibe. Again, I'm wondering if she feels what I do. I shake my head a little, answering my own question.

No. She just needed someone she trusted. But then she squeezes my hand as if silently responding to my innermost thoughts.

Turning, I see her smiling at me. I smile back as we walk up the stairs and enter the football house.

And then...we come to a screeching halt.

"Finally, you two made it!" Hendy yells, walking into the family room wearing his swim trunks, sunglasses, and a fake plastic lei. "Let's get our party on!"

Chapter Fifteen

G race

"Uh...what the hell is going on right now?"

Killian's confusion is as great as mine as we both take in the scene in the room. It's like stepping onto the set of the *Sports Illustrated* swimsuit photo shoot as guys and girls, all dressed in beach attire, meander around. I glance at my watch.

It's 4:30 in the afternoon. First, how did the day slip away so quickly? WTH? Why do we have a party happening in the house at this time of day?

Hendy slides his sunglasses to rest on top of his wet hair and actually *sees* us for the first time. His gaze travels over our bodies, brows narrowing in disgust.

"Jesus Christ! What the fuck happened to you two? Did you fall in a mud puddle or something?"

I follow his gaze, tipping my head down to get a good

look at my clothes then over at Killian. We are covered in... well, we look sickeningly gross.

"We delivered a calf," I announce proudly, offering jazz hands and a smile at Hendy, who doesn't quite seem to agree with my enthusiasm over the explanation.

He leans forward and sniffs. "So I smell..."

Hendy chuckles and waves a hand in front of his face like there's a terrible odor.

Okay, maybe he does have a point and we do smell like cows.

But you can't tell me it's worse than these guys when they return home and stash their unwashed workout clothes down in the laundry room. Now that's rancid.

"I have to say I'm impressed then," Hendy says, giving each of us a high five before hoisting his beer cup in the air in a salute. "And it calls for a drink!"

My gaze goes past the cup and out the back patio door where in the back yard there are football players, their girl-friends, some cheerleaders, and about two dozen other students. And they are all mingling around a giant slip-and-slide in the middle of the yard.

Hendy motions to the crowd behind him. "It's the Second Annual Summer Slip-and-Slide party."

When I give him a raised eyebrow, Hendy continues. "We all know this is probably the last hot day of the season, so we take advantage of the sitch and host the impromptu party."

Killian gives a resigned shrug. "That's great and all, but someone failed to notify the rest of the house"—he hooks a thumb between his chest and mine—"that it was happening right now."

"Oops," he chuckles, slamming the rest of his beer and crushing the can in his fist. "Couldn't be better timing because you two definitely need a suds and soak. For real. You two stink."

Hendy pinches his nose and scoots by us to open the cooler, grabbing a beer and heading back outside to where the crowd is cheering someone on as they run at top speed toward the slide.

I stare after Hendy who hands a guy his beer before he takes off in a run, grabbing air and flying down the slide, right into a blow-up kiddie pool filled with bubbles.

"Your friend is quite the showman." I shake my head with a laugh.

"I'm afraid so," Killian says in an apologetic shrug. And then he tips his head down to give me a serious look. "Just remember, you're the one who willingly chose to live in this house."

I crinkle my nose and nod. "Yep, I sure did. Which means..."

Taking hold of his hand, I tug him toward the back door where all the fun is being had. "This is really all Kelsie's fault and I'm blaming her for this crazy decision. Let's go swimming!"

Killian lets out a whoop of laughter as we remove most of our clothing in a flurry until we're stripped down to just our underwear. I'll probably look back on this uncharacteristically bold move and be embarrassed by my actions. But not now.

Right now I want to enjoy myself with Killian and my housemates.

The crowd outside collectively gasps over the state of our undress, but then all begin cheering in unison.

"Killer! Killer!" Hendy starts chanting and everyone joins in.

Wearing a string bikini, Lucy is sitting on top of

Emmett's lap in a lounge chair and her eyes bug out, but she joins in too. "Gracie! Gracie!"

With our hands locked again, we take a running start and throw our arms out, sailing down on our bellies over the plastic mat as we go sliding down the hill into the kiddie pool. We're covered in bubbles and soaking wet by the end. Strands of my hair stick to my face like octopus tentacles. I come up sputtering and begin laughing.

"Oh, my God! I can't believe we just did that."

"You..." He points at me, wiping water out of his eyes with the other hand. "I can't believe you just did that!"

Killian gets to his feet and offers me a hand, helping me to stand as we step out of the pool so the next people in line can take their turns. Whistles float in the air along with the bubbles and Killian's gaze settles on my wet chest. "Uh, we should probably go up and change into our swimsuits."

Tipping my head down, I now notice just how see-through my bra and panties are and find my nipples poking out from the lacy material. It looks like I'm a contestant in a wet t-shirt contest.

I quickly cover my arms over my breasts and let Killian take the lead to move in front of me so he can block everyone's view.

"Oh shit," I curse. "I'm going to regret this, aren't I?"

Killian's head spins over his shoulder and he waggles his eyebrows "But I won't."

I give him a shove with my palms against his back, the leftover bubbles dripping down to the curve of his ass. The dark pair of briefs he wears hug every part of his firm butt and tapered waist, water dripping down his thick legs.

"Oh, my God, girl. What were you guys thinking? That was crazy!"

I turn to find Lucy walking toward us, Emmett in tow.

She regards me with an expression that says I've lost my mind.

And maybe I have. Spending time with Killian at the ag center today was fun and I'm glad I got to be there to share the experience with him, even if I do smell like I was in a barn.

"And where are your clothes?"

I scan the yard to see where they may have landed and notice the pile of stinky clothes by the door.

"Our clothes were filthy because we brought a baby calf into the world today," I explain, tipping my chin up to Killian. "Not that Farm Boy really needed any help, but I assisted."

Emmett gives me an admiring grin. "Are you changing majors to become a veterinarian?"

I let out a sharp laugh. "Oh, hell no! It was absolutely disgusting. No wonder Killer smells like cow pucky all the time."

"Hey now...you don't always smell so great either." He pokes me in the side of my ribs as I try to wiggle away from him with a shriek. "Especially after that Pilates class you take. PEE-UWW!"

I notice the expressions across Lucy's and Emmett's faces. They stare at each other with a mixture of bafflement and an unspoken *I told you so* in their gazes. Hoping to get out from under their scrutinizing attention, I lift an arm and sniff at my pit.

"Yeah, okay. I definitely need to take a shower and get out of these wet clothes."

Lucy agrees with a nod of her head.

"I'll be back down in a bit."

Killian follows me as I head in through the patio doors. I stop and glance back at him over my shoulder, noticing the appreciative gaze he has plastered on my butt.

"Where do you think you're going?"

He raises his head, his dark eyes half-lidded with intent. "With you."

* * *

My heart thumps wildly in my chest and my breath is caught in my throat. The minute we ascend the stairs to the upstairs landing, I stop in the doorway to the bathroom and wait for him to make the first move.

It doesn't take long as Killian presses into my back, our bodies cool and wet, as his hands grip my biceps. His long fingers feather lightly down my arm.

Goosebumps form over every inch of my body as he leans in, his mouth at my ear, speaking in a quiet murmur. "I can't stop thinking about you, Grace."

"Me either," I confess. "I know it was only supposed to be the one time, but..." I spin around in his arms and he quirks an eyebrow. "I want to do it again with you."

"Yeah? How would that work?"

I'm confused by his question so I drop my hand to his crotch, cupping his thickening dick through the still wet briefs. Killian's eyes close on a groan.

"Well, first we get naked...and then we have sex," I joke, a smile twisting up at the corners of my mouth. "Unless you know something I don't know."

With quick reflexes, he lifts me in the air against him and a hungry growl releases from his chest. I let out a gasp at the sensation of my body pressed against his.

"I know how to do it, Soda Pop." He searches my eyes. "What I mean is, do you want this to be a regular thing?"

"Maybe..." I roll my palms over the divots and grooves of his muscular shoulders, then frame his face with my hands. "Like a roommate-with-benefits kind of thing."

His jaw tightens infinitesimally. "If that's what you want, then I'm happy to be your own personal farm boy."

I giggle against his mouth as he kisses me tentatively at first. Then the kiss grows hungry as he kicks the door shut with his heel and presses me against the bathroom wall. His firm cock aligns with my center and I tilt my pelvis to feel the hard ridge in the spot I need him most.

His lips leave mine and work their way down to the hollow of my throat. I tip my head back and allow him more room, his tongue gliding over my skin. It feels so damn good I can barely breathe.

"But I warn you..." he says against my neck, nibbling his way to my ear and then sucking my lobe between his teeth. My fingernails seek purchase as they dig into the strong cords of his neck. "You might fall in love with me."

No, I won't, I promise myself.

No matter how much I might want to, I cannot and will not fall in love.

Chapter Sixteen

K illian

It's the most perfect mixture of pain and pleasure I've ever felt.

I want Grace with every fiber of my being, but I also know she doesn't want me the same way I want her.

I'm not sure when this shift happened, but the thought of not having Grace in my life or in my bed has me twitchy.

I don't know how long I'll be able to do this roommates-with-benefits thing, but for her, I'll try.

We shower hastily, our wet, soapy hands running over each other's bodies in a hurry to get into bed. It would be easy to take her right here in the shower, fast and hard, but I want to lay her out and do everything to her. To make her come with my mouth, hands, and cock.

The deep bass beat of the music in the back yard thumps wildly, mirroring the rapid beat of my heart as I lay

Grace down. I stand at the edge of the bed, my eyes trailing down her fully naked body, followed by the slow slide of my fingertips down her middle, painting the terrain I'm going to kiss and lick before I fuck her. I stop my progress at her hip bone and stare back up into her eyes.

Our gazes lock. I don't want to tempt fate, but I need to know she's all in before I go too far.

"Are you still sure about this, soda pop?" I ask, searching her eyes for any doubts, silently begging her to say yes.

She nods, her cheeks turning pink as my finger strokes side to side just above her pubic area. "Yes."

"Good, because I'm going to make you squirm with pleasure," I vow, drawing my finger down to her wet folds, leaning in to nuzzle my nose along her neck and breathe in her fruity scent. I can smell the orange-scented soap we used and something all Grace. I smile against her flushed skin.

She whimpers and bucks her hips when I toy with her opening as if articulating the fact that she can't wait a second longer.

I shift away and look down at her again. Pressing one knee into the mattress next to her hip, I clasp my fingers into her bare thigh, stretching her leg to the side.

"This time, I'm going to tease you," I murmur before bending down and kissing the creamy flesh of her inner thigh.

"Killian, what are you doing?" she asks in a ragged whisper, reaching her hands toward my head, but I duck away. Moving up toward her head, I crash my mouth to hers in a deep, sensual kiss. She parts her lips and I intensify the kiss, our tongues tangling in the heat of our connection.

Grace lets out a small huff of protest when I end the kiss and I grin against her jaw.

"This is me taking my time," I remind her as I trail kisses along her jawline and down her neck. My fingertips trace the outline of her hip before I follow the side of her abdomen to her breast. Palming it, I run my thumb over her nipple, kissing along her collarbone.

"Killian, please. I need you inside me," she whines and the sound of her desperation almost has me giving in, especially when she punches her hips up to grind against me in search of relief. My needy girl has an insatiable appetite.

My cock leaks pre-cum and throbs like an insatiable beast too at her pleading words. But I want to ensure she gets the full experience and receives the pleasure she deserves first.

"Patience," I coo, sucking her taut nipple into my mouth and flicking it with a roll of my tongue. "You'll like this, I promise."

When I alternate licking and sucking on one nipple before making sure I pay the same homage to the other, her hands dive into my hair, nails raking over my scalp. It's a biting pain that I like, so I continue my ministrations, bringing her higher and higher, closer to the edge of sanity.

Once she's squirming beneath me, I continue my descent with wet kisses to her stomach. Circling my tongue around her belly button, I toy with both breasts until she lets out a low moan, her fingers still wrapped in my hair. She's trembling slightly, her hips moving and shifting against the mattress. She knows what she wants from me, but I want to hear her say it.

"What do you want, soda pop?" I tease, smirking against the soft skin of her belly.

"You know what I want," she mutters, letting out a grunt of frustration.

I chuckle and settle myself between her thighs, blowing

lightly over her swollen sex. She wriggles and fidgets. I bite the soft flesh of her inner thigh, knowing I'm driving her crazy with lust.

"Stop teasing me, Killer!"

"Do you want something?" I ask again, nipping at her inner thigh with a smile.

She glares down at me and I grin, gently pressing my thumbs at her folds to spread her open for me.

With the exception of a small gasp, Grace remains quiet, her eyes following me as I lean forward, my own gaze locked with hers. I glide the tip of my tongue over her clit, savoring her taste while I watch her pupils dilate. Her legs tremble and quiver at my touch. Her scent and taste have me trembling for more.

And suddenly I'm not so sure I can keep my shit together long enough to take it as slow as I want to.

If I remain in this position, I'm liable to crawl up her body and slide inside. So instead, I move up the bed and lie next to her, my head against the headboard. She turns her face toward me and gives me an inquisitive look.

"Come here." I wiggle my fingers, gesturing for her to come closer. She purses her lips together with uncertainty. "I want you to sit on my face. Right now."

She lets out a laugh, eyebrows shooting upward. "You're joking."

I roll to my side and with my hands on her hips, I lift her body, her legs straddling my chest. "I promise you, I'm very serious."

I give her a second to settle her knees on each side of my head, and I slip my palms under her ass, positioning her closer to my mouth.

"Hang on to the headboard, Grace. You're gonna need leverage."

"But...I don't...won't I...how will you breathe?" she stammers awkwardly, trying to resist my attempts to latch on. I dig my heels into the bed and scoot down a few more inches until I'm directly underneath her center, just a mere inch from her pussy.

"Sweetness, if I'm not near death from lack of oxygen after eating you out, I'm doing this all fucking wrong."

My grip tightens on her hips and I drag her pussy down to my lips, my nose bumping her clit as my tongue finds her entrance. It takes all of three seconds and several laps of my tongue for her to finally get the hang of it. But fucking hell... when she does, Grace rides me like a rodeo champ.

"Oh, shit, Killian...please don't stop."

I'm a man on a mission to ensure she comes so hard she's seeing stars. While sucking on her clit, I slowly work a finger, and then two, inside of her, easing them in and out as she rocks against me.

Within a few seconds, I feel her inner walls seizing with small tremors and I slide my tongue inside. I want to taste all of her.

"I'm so close," she murmurs, her hips undulating over me. The shy timid nature she had a moment ago is quickly replaced by feral need. She's grinding against my face and hot little moans slip from her lips. Suddenly, she is all I hear.

All I feel is Grace.

All I smell is Grace.

All I taste is Grace.

And all I see is Grace.

She completely owns my senses.

If I'm being honest, Grace completely owns me.

I double my efforts and a moment later, Grace cries out her release, her thighs quivering around my ears, her breaths coming out in fast pants as I lap up the sweet remnants of her orgasm.

Grace falls forward, her forehead pressed against the frame of the bed, barely holding herself upright. I bite the inside of her thigh before I slowly ease out from underneath her. She's panting hard and her body looks like it's about to collapse. I pat the pillow next to me and she falls to her side, our faces inches apart.

"How was that?" I ask, cupping her cheeks in my hand.

She blinks slowly and then a slow, languorous smile spreads across her mouth.

"Wow...that was..."

"See? I told you I'd make it good." I drop my hand to her shoulder and then run my fingertips down to her hip, smoothing them over the curve of her ass. Experimenting a little, I drag a finger through the crease of her ass, my finger coated in her wetness.

"Oh fuck, babe. You're so wet."

I take my dick in hand, using her moisture as lubricant to pump my shaft in my fist as Grace observes with half-lidded eyes. I peer over at her.

"Wanna help?"

"Yes, please," she begs breathlessly. I reach for her hand and place it over my straining cock as we set a rhythm together. It's slow at first, but builds and climbs until I have to stop before I come all over her hand.

"What's wrong? Didn't you like that?" Grace asks when I remove her hand from my erection.

Shifting to my side, I pull her in close and kiss her lips. "It was amazing. But I want to come when I'm buried inside all this tight wet heat of yours." My hand slides between her legs again and she moans.

"Can we...you know...try it from behind?"

I raise an interested eyebrow. "Are you asking me to fuck you doggie style?" The thought nearly has me coming right this second from not only the suggestion, but also from her gorgeous and shy grin. She nods.

"As you wish." I chuckle, flipping her onto her knees and tugging at her ankles to bring her to the edge of the bed where I settle in behind her. "Now hang on."

Taking my cock in hand, I rub the tip against her wet pussy. I grow harder with every pass through her folds until I can no longer take it anymore and slide into her entrance.

Our moans mingle as I push in, inch by inch, enjoying the exquisite feel of her pussy contracting around me until I'm finally buried to the hilt. We both let out a sigh of relief the minute we're joined completely.

My hand roams down her back and her head drops to the mattress, the angle creating an even deeper sensation. I begin to move languidly in and out, tentative but eager.

"You won't break me, Killian," she insists, looking over her shoulder. "Harder, farm boy."

A moan escapes her lips when I begin to thrust harder and with more force.

"Fuck, yeah, babe. You have no idea how good you feel."

I do it again and again, setting a punishing pace, slamming in and out until I feel her inner muscles clench around my dick.

"Mmm...I do."

And that's all it takes for me to lose my control as I begin to thrust hard and fast. Her body trembles and she cries out my name as I come on a grunt.

"Fuck," I bellow, my balls tighten and then explode as I orgasm, spilling inside her.

Enjoying our connection, I hold on to her hips without pulling out. Being inside her and feeling every inch of her heat wrapped around me has awoken some primitive part of me and I never want to pull out. I want to stay inside her like this forever.

But slowly I grab the base of my cock and step backwards. The view when I look down at her bent position has me getting hard again already.

"Do you have any fucking idea how hot you look right now?" I watch in awe as the evidence of my orgasm runs down her thigh.

I place my other hand on the small of her back to keep her in that position.

"Stay there. I'll go get a towel to clean you up."

When I return from the bathroom, Grace is in the same position, her pert ass in the air, her face to the side and pressed into the mattress. She gives me a sideways look as I gently wipe at the insides of her thighs and then between her legs with a damp cloth.

"All good," I say, throwing the towel in the dirty clothes hamper and climbing into bed next to her. She snuggles into my chest with a dreamy sigh.

"That was..."

"Pretty fucking amazing. I know."

She nods against my chest. "Is it always this good? No, don't tell me. I don't want to know what I've been missing out on for this long."

Chuckling, I wrap my arm more tightly around her waist and stroke my thumb under the smooth skin of her breast.

"Honestly, It's not always this good," I admit, thinking back on what I used to believe was good sex. That was then and this is now. "There has to be chemistry. You and me... it's hard to explain, but we definitely have it."

She throws an arm over my chest and burrows against

my side, pressing a kiss to my chin before laying her head back down.

"I'm glad it's with you, Killian. I feel like...I can trust you."

I give her a squeeze. The sound of my phone pinging with a text interrupts the moment, but I ignore it in favor of enjoying this time with Grace.

"You can trust me, soda pop. I promise."

I just wish she wanted more from me than trust. I wish she wanted it all.

Chapter Seventeen

G race

It's Friday afternoon and I'm sprawled out on my bed trying to study for an upcoming exam, but my mind is on anything but school stuff.

Okay, it's on Killian.

There's a football game tomorrow night, so Killian and the guys have an extra practice today, otherwise he'd be here in bed with me. And we'd be talking, fooling around, or having sex. Or all of the above. We're really good at it all.

I'm lying flat on my stomach with my laptop and books open, scrolling through my phone, but I am too distracted to read anything. I know I should be studying and working on my research project, but I keep replaying the other night in my head. When he took me from behind and it was so freaking good.

Like, I thought I'd be nervous and embarrassed about it because, you know...he's staring at my butt in the air.

But it was nothing like that. It was the most amazing thing ever. I can still feel his rough palms holding my hips securely in place as he set a perfect tempo. And the slide of his cock inside me as his hand wandered over the length of my back, sent shivers up and down my spine. Hitting me so deep that I swore I could feel him in my womb.

All of it paled in comparison, though, afterwards when he took such sweet care of me, cleaning me up and holding me in his arms.

I never expected something seemingly so awkward to feel so comfortable.

My face flops down into the pillow and I inhale a deep breath. Well, shit. That doesn't help matters at all because I can still smell him on my pillow. It smells of spice and soap, and something all Killian.

I'm not sure when this happened, but the annoying roommate from earlier this semester and the guy who was just supposed to take my virginity has turned into a guy I may be falling for.

Or maybe I already have.

The thought scares me shitless.

Which means, I need advice from the man expert. The one and only Kelsie Dannon. The one who went off to France over the summer and stayed to study abroad. If it weren't for her, I wouldn't be in this predicament in the first place so I figure she owes me.

I roll over and pick up my phone, pulling up her contact info to FaceTime her. I'm not even sure what time it is in Paris right now, but dammit, she needs to help me sort through this mess with Killian.

If it's one thing I know and love about Kelsie, it's that

she's an independent, worldly woman who lets guys into her bed, but would never let a guy break her heart.

The video screen pops up as I hold the phone over my head in front of my face. Two rings and a smaller screen illuminates and *voila*, there is my beautiful best friend right in front of me as if she weren't five thousand miles away.

"*Bonjour, mademoiselle!*" Kelsie greets, sounding very Parisian and giving me air kisses with a very French flair. She looks to be wearing a pair of coveralls and has paint splotches over her face and neck. Upon closer inspection, I notice she even has green paint in her hair.

"Hey, Sugar Smacks. What is going on with your face?" I gesture with a circle over my own face.

"Hey, Honey Bunches of Oats," she retorts, using the nickname she gave me our freshman year. "What's going on with mine? It's only some paint. I can't say the same thing about yours, though. You're disgusting to look at." She makes a fake gagging sound and I laugh, flipping her my middle finger in view of the camera.

God, it's good to see her. It hasn't been as frequent as I'd like or thought it would be. I suppose that's what happens when your BFF is on the other side of the world.

It's not that I don't love living here with Lucy and that she's not also my best friend, it's that I miss Kelsie's wicked sense of humor and the way she can make light of any situation.

The girl has no trouble being real and talking smack, which is why I started calling her Sugar Smacks in the first place. And, in turn, she named me Honey Bunches of Oats. That's because she says I'm sweet and wholesome. Or was at the time.

I guess she better find a different name to use for me

now. I'm not as innocent as I was before she left the country.

Which is why I need to talk to her. I need her to give me a pep talk so I can find a way out of falling in love with Killian.

Kelsie has been with a ton of guys over the years. They fall at her feet and worship her like some goddess. And I get it. She's a gorgeous SoCal girl who has that carefree artist vibe and is passionate about life. She says that's because her element sign is fire.

I roll over to prop myself on my elbows and steady the phone against my headboard. The same headboard I gripped tightly when Killian and I were...

"Spill the tea, girl. Something's going on with you." Kelsie accuses, pointing the end of a paint brush at me and spinning it around. "I can see it written all over that disgustingly beautiful face of yours."

I sigh and scrunch my nose—she's so damn intuitive.

I take a deep breath and let it all out in a gust of air. "I've been sleeping with someone."

I leave out the part that he also took my virginity. We don't need to open up that can of worms.

Kelsie would be so mad to learn I hadn't confided in her about still being a virgin until recently. For all she knows, I lost it years ago. I may share it with Lucy at some point if it ever comes up, but Kelsie would really be butt hurt. She'd see it as an insult that I didn't trust in her enough to be honest about it.

She has a tendency to be like that. It's all or nothing with her, especially with those she loves. She cut off her own brother because of something he did to her years ago.

Kelsie's face brightens and her mouth gapes open.

"*Wwwwhaaaat?* You mean, you're sleeping with the same guy? On the reg?"

I giggle, feeling myself blush. "Um, yeah."

"Okay, hold the phone. I need to put this shit away, grab my wine, and sit down to have a proper chat. You need to tell me *everything*."

She takes a few seconds to organize her paint supplies as the camera follows her around the large, coffered ceiling, vintage-looking studio. It's in the Montmartre apartment her aunt owns and put Kelsie up in while she's away in Spain. Her aunt, Desiree La Mona, is a famed artist who achieved glory when she sold some paintings to the royal family in England. Her career took off and ever since she's been living in France.

It is Kelsie's dream to follow in her footsteps and work and deal in the art world. But she knows she first has to get her undergrad in International Studies to appease her dad, who said he'd cut her off if she didn't graduate with a degree.

Kelsie comes back into view again and is sitting cross-legged on a plush lavender couch, her bib overalls pulled down to expose a black tank underneath. The paint is still caked on her face, which makes her look younger and cute.

She takes a fortifying sip of some red wine and nods. "I'm all ears. Now tell me all the deets about this guy you've been boning. He must have a magic D. Who is he?"

Well, here goes...I take a long breath and exhale.

"It's Killian."

As if I'd just reached through the phone and slapped her, Kelsie's face morphs into a comical mixture of confusion, disgust, and incredulous disbelief.

There's a long pause.

Kelsie's voice raises a few octaves. "You mean Killian, as

in Killer? Your stinky, loud-mouthed, dirty farmer boy, football player roommate you complained about not even a month ago?"

I arch my brows and lift a coy shoulder.

"Yeah, that one. Although, to his credit, he does shower and do his laundry more often now." And I love how he smells, but I don't say that.

Kelsie busts out laughing, clearing the air, and I chuckle along with her.

"Oh, my fucking God! Gracie! You're not supposed to sleep with your roommate. Haven't I taught you anything?" She tips back her wine glass and takes a healthy sip before shaking her head. "That could get messy."

Not if I don't fall in love. I just nod.

"I know, but it won't. We're just hooking up. But I kinda need to ask you about that."

Her thick, dark blonde eyebrows furrow inward.

"About what? I've never slept with one of my roommates," she teases, giving me a pointed look. She leans back against the side of the velvet couch and stretches out her legs across it. I flip to my side, propping my head up with my palm.

"How do you keep your feelings, you know, out of the equation? Because the sex is really good, but I kind of like him too."

Kelsie slaps her palm against her forehead and rolls her eyes.

"See? This is what I'm talking about. If you hook-up with a guy more than five times, it becomes a *relationship*." She uses air quotes and crinkles her nose. "That's when it can move into dangerous territory. I've avoided that at all costs."

I do some quick calculations in my head. "But weren't

you sleeping with that frat boy last year for at least a few months?"

Kelsie turns her head away, not meeting my gaze, her mouth curved in a mischievous smile.

"I may have moved on to another guy in the house after what's-his-name," she admits, turning back to face me.

I arch my brows and she lifts her shoulders innocently. "What? I like variety. I got bored with him so I hooked up with one of his frat brothers. So sue me."

I snort loudly. "Oh, Kels, I miss you. It's not the same without you here."

She smiles demurely and flicks the side of her hair. "I know. I'm special like that. And if I were there, I'd still tell you the same thing. Use protection. Have fun. And don't fucking fall in love."

I've checked off two on the list at least.

She must see something flash in my eyes because she leans closer to the camera, stares at my face, and groans. "Oh shit, Gracie. You have, haven't you?"

I throw my head down into the pillow and hide my face. "I don't know," I whisper. "Maybe?"

She sighs wearily. "I suppose it had to happen eventually. But why Killer? Ugh..."

Just then, the door to our bedroom swings open abruptly and I spring off the mattress and the phone goes flying onto the bed as Killian barges inside.

"I heard my name so here I am!" he announces with a goofy, cheesy smile. Then he throws himself on the bed and tackles me. He catches himself on his arms to prop him up so he doesn't crush me with the weight of his body. I scream and giggle, forgetting all about the phone until we hear Kelsie yelling at us.

"Knock it off! I do *not* want to see that shit."

Killian pops up and reaches for the phone, bringing it to his face to make kissy noises at it.

"Hi, Kelsieeeee!" he sing-songs. "Bye, Kelsieeeee!"

And then he disconnects the call and cages me in with his hands on both sides of my body. He's warm and smells clean and fresh, his hair still damp from his after-practice shower.

He stops abruptly and his eyes widen guiltily.

"Uh-oh. I didn't just let out our secret, did I?"

We'd both committed to keeping our hookups private for now, not wanting to get our housemates involved in knowing all our intimate details. So we'd kept it to ourselves and haven't shared it with anyone yet. Until now.

I swing my arms around his neck, locking my heels at his lower back.

"Nah, it's all good. Kelsie knows about us, but she won't say anything. Plus, she's in France. What's she gonna do about it?"

"Absolutely nothing," he agrees, making me forget everything else except the way he tastes when he kisses me. His mouth crashes over mine in a devouring kiss and he sinks into me and takes my breath away.

Maybe this is what love feels like? So what if I'm falling for him?

It feels a whole lot better than anything else I've ever experienced before. And I don't want to let it go.

At least, not yet.

Chapter Eighteen

K illian

She's falling in love with me.

I know what I heard when she was on the phone with Kelsie and I want to believe it.

Goddamn, I want it to be true because I feel like I've been falling for her more with each passing day, hoping she'd catch up. I know she was adamant initially about not wanting a relationship, but maybe I've somehow broken through her defenses.

I pull back from kissing her and gaze down into her eyes.

"You're back early," she says softly, a sweet grin lighting up her face.

I return the grin. "I am. We did great on our drills, so the coach let us out a few minutes early."

"Are you ready for the game tomorrow?"

I nod and roll us over so she's straddling me and my cock is wedged perfectly between her legs. My hand inches under her t-shirt and I run my thumb over the exposed skin on her abdomen. "It'll be tough, but I'm ready. Tomorrow's going to be a long day."

"I bet," she agrees as she leans forward and plants a kiss on my mouth. Pulling back a little, I feel her grin against my lips. "Maybe I can help you...relax."

Grace's fingers make their way down to my stomach and she begins to undo my pants, burrowing her hand inside and wrapping around my growing erection.

"You're insatiable, soda pop." I let out a low groan.

"It's all your fault," she teases. "You keep giving it to me."

I buck my hips upward playfully. "Oh, I'll give you something alright."

She giggles and slips off her leggings and underwear and then returns her hands to my rigid cock, stroking me so tightly I practically come on the spot. I should try to slow things down so we can talk about what I heard her say, but it feels so good when she slides her wet folds along the length of my dick that I forget all about the discussion topic.

Grace takes the lead and I let her do her thing, shoving my hands behind my head to watch her take control. To watch her work me over and find a rhythm that feels good for her as she rocks over my steely erection. Finally, she throws her head back and her body quivers as she comes so perfectly above me.

I'm soon close to the edge myself, so I flip her onto her back, maneuvering between her legs and penetrating her entrance before thrusting in hard and fast. Grace gasps in pleasure when I bottom out and I stop for a moment to enjoy the incredible sensation of being inside her.

It takes me four strokes and I'm throwing my own head back in and growling out my release.

Fuck, it's never felt this good before. It just keeps getting better and better every time I'm inside Grace.

I don't move for a long moment afterward, trying to identify the mess of emotions that float around in my head and heart.

While my dick is still buried deep inside her, I stare down into her warm brown eyes, glazed with an afterglow.

"I'm falling in love with you, soda pop," I offer quietly, even though my heart is exploding loudly.

Grace blinks, her face growing pale and I watch with fascination as her throat contracts and she swallows audibly.

"And I think you might feel the same way."

She doesn't readily return the sentiment, and I search her eyes for an answer, hoping to hear the same. Will she admit her feelings to me?

Time seems to move slowly and when she doesn't answer, I pull out and roll to my side, propping myself up against her headboard. Normally after sex, Grace will snuggle against me. But this time, it's like she's turned to cold stone. She doesn't move for a time and when she finally does, she sits up and stares down at her legs, avoiding my gaze.

"I...I'm sorry, Killian, but this,"—she motions between us—"it's just about sex for me."

I lean toward her. "You're lying," I say, my jaw clenched. "That's bullshit."

"No, it's not. I'm sorry we're not on the same page, but I thought you understood."

I climb out of her bed, pulling my pants back up from where they were pushed down to my ankles and turn to face her, angry and hurt because I know she's not telling me the truth.

But what can I do? Maybe I'll have to cut her off and see how she reacts.

"Fine. If that's how you feel, then we're done with this. I'm not going to be your fuck toy to use."

"Killian, please." Her eyes fill with tears. "You know you're not."

I hold up a hand and notice it's shaking with anger. "Not now, Grace. If you don't want to have an honest conversation about what's going on here, then we shouldn't have one at all."

She turns away and stares down at her hands in her lap.

Fine. If I mean so little to her that she doesn't want to discuss things, so be it. I'll go focus on my homework.

I forcefully drag the curtain closed behind me with a loud, satisfying snick, essentially blocking Grace out of my space, but not out of my mind.

Breathing heavily, I sit down at my desk, open my laptop, and pull up a file for a paper I'm writing on sustainable food systems and farming. I need to finish my first draft by tomorrow to submit to the TA for feedback. But instead, I'm attuned to every little sound coming from the other side of the curtain.

How am I supposed to concentrate? Her scent still lingers on me and I don't want to wash it off.

I'm about to march my ass back to her side of the room and confront her again about why she's so stubborn and resistant about there being an official *us* when my phone buzzes.

> Big Guy: Hey son, call me when you get a chance.

I frown. It's from my dad, who is generally not a big phone talker unless it's birthdays or holidays. He's the strong and silent type. His way of showing his love for us is to take us horseback riding or fishing in the pond. The fact that he wants me to call him so out of the blue is a little alarming, so I decide to go find a quiet place to return the call.

Leaving our room, where the scent of sex still lingers, I head downstairs and out to the front porch. It's quiet here this time of the evening and I call my dad who answers on the first ring.

"Hey," he says, his voice sounding a bit strained and I immediately can tell something isn't right just from the way he says that single word.

"What's wrong?"

He sighs deeply. "Oh, just having some trouble with the inventory and getting the right amounts shipped to the right locations. It's nothing too big, but a hassle nonetheless."

Our dairy farm has been struggling for a while. These days, we're competing with so many other varieties of dairies and from other sources of milk. It's not just one dairy farmer against the other. It's now the hemp, the almond, the coconut, the soy. You name it, it's never-ending. And it also means we've had to find other methods of getting production costs down. If we don't, we'll not be able to stay in the game much longer.

It's the reason I've been using the problem in developing my independent research project topic, to help me brainstorm some marketing ideas that could eventually lead to increased sales. If we can't even get the inventory and shipping stuff right, though, then I'm behind the eight ball.

"Are the shitheads doing their part?" I ask, referring to my brothers, who should be helping my dad.

"Killian," Dad scolds. "That's not the issue here."

"Well, are they?" I prod, some of my residual anger from my fight with Grace spilling over into this. I swear my parents gave all the responsibility to me and let those two jackoffs mess around half the time.

"Yes. Everyone is working hard, son. It's just difficult to get part-time help this time of year when everyone goes back to school, so it's an adjustment and I'm spending more time with the bottling and packing," Dad explains.

And even though he doesn't mean to, his words feel aimed at me and guilt rides up in my throat. Because I'm the one who left to go back to school, leaving them to pick up the slack.

My dad continues, "I'm trying to figure out some way to make all of this more efficient, but I was hoping you could brainstorm with me. I could use some of that college smarts you got, kid."

"Maybe I can come home for a few days." I mentally calculate the time it takes to drive home to Iowa and if I can fit it in around my football games and schedule. I could easily be gone for four days without missing a thing.

"No, son. You're too busy. You need to stay there where you belong."

Sighing, I run a hand over my face. It sucks being so far away from my family sometimes. It's like my heart is in two places—here and there. And right now it's in pieces here.

"I'll do my best to come up with something, Dad. I promise. Just give me some time. I won't let you down."

"Thanks, kid. So how's school going by the way? Are you playing tomorrow?" Dad asks, knowing my team's game schedule. If we have televised games, he and the entire town will be watching and rooting me on from afar. I miss home.

"Yep. That's the plan," I say, the game the furthest thing

from my mind right now. Between what happened with Grace and now the worry over the farm and business, I'm not sure I can add another thing to my plate.

"Well, you know we'll all be watching."

"Thanks, Dad." I can't ignore the tug in my heart.

"Gotta go. Larry Hartman is stopping by with extra hay. Apparently, his wife over-ordered so we're buying some off him."

"Okay, cool. I'll talk to you soon, Dad," I add before we disconnect. Suddenly, my mind is on my family and not on the irritating situation with the sexy woman in my bedroom. I don't have time to push Grace into confessing she has feelings for me. Or delve into why she won't admit it and is resistant to move forward with something.

I head back upstairs and sit down at my desk, ignoring the need to check in on Grace. And as much as I want to get online and play video games right now to distract me from everything, I need to try to figure out this issue for my dad. But when I open my laptop, there's a notification from the message app on *Capital Offense*.

I decide to check it first before I get back into my paper or start the project I have in mind for the farm.

Opening the chat box, I smile at the message from my gamer friend.

RanchHandRAM1: Yo, you've been MIA. I miss playing against you. Mostly because you suck balls and are a lousy player, and I can beat your ass every time.

RanchHandRAM1: Things here have been kinda weird in my life. Kinda been seeing someone and it was good for a while. Now I'm not so sure.

RanchHandRAM1: Anyway, hope you're okay and I'll see you online sometime soon.

I'm about to respond, seeing as the chat message came in only a few minutes earlier, but remind myself of the deadlines I need to meet. So rather than get sucked into the chat, I minimize the screen and open my paper.

Then I hear Grace on the other side of the Great Divide, the sound of her clickity-clack typing on her keyboard grating on my nerves. I swear with each tap of a key, I grow more annoyed with her. She's giving me whiplash. Why would she say those things to Kelsie and then turn around and deny it, telling me the exact opposite?

God, women!

I don't think Emmett had this much trouble with Lucy before they started dating for real. Then again, they were only pretending in the first place.

This thing between Grace and me is one-hundred percent fucking real. Or at least I thought it was until an hour ago.

I stew over all of this for the next few hours, headphones in and nose buried in my work. But by nine, I'm growing hungry and decide to give it up for a bit to go get some grub, shower, and then force myself to sleep. Tomorrow is going to be a long day, and the more I think about it, the more I believe I need to head home for a few days.

If I play in the game tomorrow and leave right after, it'd be a long night of driving, but I could get there by sunrise. It's not the first time I've driven all night. And besides the paper, which I can submit online, I don't have anything huge on my class schedules next week, so missing a few days won't be a big deal.

Plus, it will give me some distance from and perspective on Grace. Maybe that will help us both. Maybe it's just space we need right now.

I contemplate telling Grace that I'll be gone for a few days as I'm downstairs making a sandwich. I mean, I should tell her, right? She is my roommate after all.

After finishing my sandwich, I jump in the shower, spending time under the spray to let my mind wander. Just this afternoon I was deep inside Grace's body, the closest you can ever be with a person. And now it feels like the continental divide is between us.

As I lay back down in bed, I hear her over in hers, the sheets rustling as if she's restless.

It takes all my willpower not to get up, open the curtain, and demand we talk through this. Then again, maybe a few days apart will be good for us.

If I go home, it's possible I'll realize that I'm not actually in love with Grace. It's just the physical proximity to her that has me believing that story.

I shove my head into my pillow and groan softly. Goddamn, she's so frustrating!

Why did I let her talk me into taking her virginity? Into sleeping with her like I'm her personal on-demand booty call? And why does she need to play it so cool?

My phone pings with a text and I pick up the phone off the charger to see who it's from.

> Hendy: You up? Wanna come down and play?

I consider his request and then whip off the sheet from my legs.

Me: Hell yes. I'll be down in a minute.

Might as well blow off some steam with my friend. It beats lying here and replaying every conversation and every intimate moment I've had with Grace over the last few months.

I'm hoping an hour or two playing video games with Hendy will help me sort out my life.

Who am I kidding? It won't help at all, but at least it will provide a good distraction, as will the drive home tomorrow night.

The drive after a game will be brutal, but at the very least it will leave me and my brain alone in my truck to work out some shit.

And maybe putting several hundred miles between Grace and me will be the best thing for us both.

Chapter Nineteen

Grace

I'm so angry right now I could scream. The sad truth of the matter is that I'm angry with myself, not with Killian.

When he said he loved me, instead of returning the sentiment, I choked up. I denied it. Denied it out of fear.

I've seen what happens when love goes south. I've seen how it divides loyalties. Breaks hearts. Ruins families.

Hurts children.

It's what happened between my mom and dad, leaving me dangling between them like a rag doll, pulled in opposite directions until I stopped resisting and became what they both wanted from me. A daughter who would be compliant and not take sides.

I resisted the urge to run back to Killian's side and tell him the truth about my feelings.

Yes, I love you! You're the best guy I've ever known.

But I couldn't admit to any of that without breaking down. So I bottled it up and focused on my game. Or tried to, at least.

Once I heard Killian leave the room, I started messaging my online friend, the only way I had to vent at the moment because Lucy was at a tutoring session tonight. Plus, she and Emmett don't know anything yet about what's been going on between me and Killian.

Sadly, I've gotten no response from my online friend yet, even after sending a few messages. I feel utterly alone.

> RanchHandRAM1: Hey, you there? Your status says you are.

> I need advice.

> Have you ever been in a relationship? (And no, I'm not talking about your own hand or asking you to get involved with me, so don't even go there.) I like this person, but don't want to admit it.

> Hello? Are my messages going into thin air?

I throw my headphones off in a huff and they land on the bed with a small bounce. At the same time, I hear the ding of a message over on Killian's side of the room. Hmmm. Weird. He must've left his laptop open.

There are several more dings from behind the curtain and they make me curious. Who is messaging him?

Probably the guys. Or maybe he's already on the prowl for other girls?

A sharp pain like I've never felt before slices through my gut, just as if I were my avatar in *Capital Offense* and a sword was shoved into my abdomen by an opponent.

My jealousy wins out and I throw my legs over the side of my bed. As if I'm on a secret mission and don't want to be caught, I quietly tiptoe to the curtain, easing it back to reveal Killian's side of the attic.

I'm surprised to see it's relatively clean, even by my standards. Killian has been far more conscientious of his mess now that we're sleeping together. It's one of the many things I've come to appreciate about him, not to mention how good he is at making me feel special.

Some of my frustration subsides as I creep over to his desk, finding his laptop open and a gaming site up.

There's a paused background where it looks like he'd been about to play before getting pulled into something else. There's also a recognizable blue chat box at the right bottom screen.

The same blue box in my game.

I lean down and notice the unread messages of the open chat.

What in the actual fuck?

They're the messages I just sent to **BigHardware69**.

I stagger back and blink hard, trying to comprehend what is going on. Is Killian my online friend in *Capital Offense?*

Before I have a chance to investigate further, another message pops up but it's not in the game's chat box. It's a notification on *WhatsApp*.

It's a message from Big Guy.

Hey son,

Just following up. It was great talking to you. I'm sorry I dumped all that shit on you about the farm business because I know you're swamped. But I'd sure appreciate it if you could look through these numbers I've attached and come up with a tracking mechanism. It might make this easier to manage. I'd love to see what you come up with. Whatever you can do, I'd appreciate it.

> Love you, son. We all miss you and are proud of you.
>
> Dad

My heart sinks to my shoes. Killian never mentioned anything about his dad's farm being in trouble. Or at least, that's the way it sounds if Mr. Palmer is asking for his son's help to come up with a way to fix things.

There's an attached spreadsheet and the wheels in my head start moving on fast rotation. Without giving it a second thought, I click on the spreadsheet, saving a copy before sending it to my email. The message is being delivered just as I hear someone coming up the stairs.

I whirl around, my heart caught in my throat, flinging the curtain back in place and jumping on my bed before there's a knock on the door.

The relief is palpable. It's one thing to be in a fight with Killian, but to get caught snooping in his computer? That wouldn't be something he could easily forgive.

Guilt washes over me as I wonder if I've done the right thing.

"Are you still awake in there?" Lucy asks quietly as she opens the door a crack to let the hallway light in.

"Yep, come on in."

She strides in with a cheery smile on her face. This is the glow of a woman in love. I couldn't be happier for her and EJ. They are a perfect match and absolutely a couple goal. If only I could let Killian in, like Lucy has with Emmett, with no fear of abandonment, I would do it without hesitation.

Not uttering so much as a word, she heads over to my closet and peers inside, sifting through the racks of my clothing before turning her head over her shoulder.

"Hey, can I borrow that hot pink top you wore last week? It was so cute."

I stand behind her and reach in to extract it from the far back of my closet. It's in my rotation, and since I recently wore it, it's placed in the back of the closet. This is a trick Kelsie taught me our freshman year.

Lifting it from the hanger, I hold out my hand to offer it to her. Lucy grabs it, examining it in front of her chest with interest.

"Do you think it'll look good on me?"

"Yeah, it goes great with your complexion," I say, thumbing through some other clothes on the closet shelf in search of the skinny jeans I paired with it. Finding the pair, I hold them up. "You want to wear these too?"

Her eyes go wide. "Oooh, can I?"

"Of course," I agree, but then tuck them behind my back and tilt my head. "As long as you tell me what you need these for."

Lucy's cheeks flood with her typical blush and she looks away. "It's our nine month anniversary and Emmett's taking me out after the game tomorrow night."

I can't help but coo. "Awww...that's so sweet. You two are adorbs."

"I know."

She says it with such dreamy emphasis. Not in a boastful way, just matter-of-factly.

I go in search of the silver earrings I wore with the outfit to add to the ensemble as she sits on the end of the bed.

"How about you and Killian? Are you ever going to announce it and officially move past the friends-with-bennies thing into the dating scene yet?"

I twirl around in shock. "What? How did you know?"

Lucy bursts out in laughter. "Grace, we are literally right underneath this attic. You don't think we hear you two fucking like bunnies?"

Casting my eyes downward, I avoid her eye contact. "Are you mad I didn't tell you?"

She pats the bed next to her and I take a seat, placing the earrings in her palm.

"I'm sorry I didn't tell you. We were trying to keep it a secret. Plus, it doesn't matter now because we're in a huge fight at the moment."

Lucy lets out a short gasp. "Oh, no. What happened?"

"I'm an idiot, that's what happened."

She laughs dryly. "Very doubtful. Anyway, it's usually the guy's fault, isn't it?"

"Not in this case. It was all me."

I fill Lucy in on what's been going on between me and Killian and about the discussion—or lack of discussion— around our relationship status. Leaving out my reservations about love, I explain it's just not what I want right now.

Lucy gives me an empathetic look. "Well, you can't force yourself to feel something that isn't there. If it's not right, then it's not. But damn, girl. Killian looks at you like you hung the freaking stars."

My stomach somersaults and then knots into a pretzel. I know what look she's referring to.

It's the look he gives me when we're in bed together, talking about school or life or our futures. It's the gentle way he gazes at me when he brushes the hair out of my eyes or kisses my eyelashes so softly they feel like angel kisses.

Which is the reason why I've decided to develop a software program for his family to use for the farm. After seeing the message from his dad, I want to do something to help them out so they don't lose everything they've worked for. It'll be my way of apologizing to Killian for not being able to give him what he wants.

I may not be able to tell him I love him right now, but at least I can show him in the only way I know how.

Chapter Twenty

K illian

I gulp down my fourth energy drink. I've been on the road for over two hours after a very physical game on the field, and I still have a good six hours to go before I reach the farm.

I wouldn't be on the road at all had it not been for my teammate Nathan, who also had to leave after the game and needed a ride a few towns over. General rule is that the entire team rides the bus for away games, mostly for team continuity and camaraderie.

But in this case, Coach agreed prior to our bus leaving the campus that Nathan could leave after the game if he had a ride because of a family thing and then reluctantly let me drive him when I explained it was an emergency at home. It might not be the whole truth, and it's not like anyone's in the hospital, but it still feels like an emergency to me.

Dad clearly needs my help.

I remember what EJ said when I told him I was leaving with Nathan.

"What? You gotta be kidding me? We just beat the motherfucking Eagles! You had one of the best receptions and yardage I've seen from you all season," EJ says, patting me on the back. "You have to come out and celebrate this win with us."

I groan. "How can you be happy when I totally fumbled that pass in the second half?" I point out as I stuff my dirty things into my duffle bag. The memory of the ball slipping through my hands is far too fresh and left an indelible mark on my mood. Add that to everything else I'm dealing with.

"Whatever. You played well. You just seemed...in your head tonight," he says as he sits down next to my bag on the bench, our teammates chatting and packing up their bags around us.

We're booked in the hotel tonight in Eastmount, with the bus leaving early tomorrow morning. But the buzz coming from everyone's mouths sounds like there will be some major partying happening with all the students and friends who made the trek over here for the game. Hendy's standing in the corner of the locker room, holding court while talking to a sports reporter. He's throwing a fake ball, showing how he makes the perfect spiral pass.

EJ shakes his head, hooking a thumb at our star quarterback. "Hendy was on fire tonight."

I nod. "He was. Those passes were incredible," I agree and zip up my bag.

"You ready, Nathan?" I call out, throwing my bag over my shoulder.

He walks over and grins, holding out his phone for us to see a picture of a newborn baby. He kind of looks like a wrinkly alien.

"I missed out on seeing him born. But hopefully I can get there in a few hours, thanks to Killer, and meet my new nephew," he says with a proud smile.

"Well, he's cute. I'm ready to roll when you are."

"Everything okay?" EJ asks, walking with me toward the door.

I shrug. "It will be. I'll be back in a few days. You guys have a celebratory drink for me."

It was hard to turn down the after-game celebration with the guys. I know I only have a few more times to do that this season and then it's my last year.

The only silver lining to my already shitty weekend is that we beat the Eagles, one of the best teams in our division this year, so it puts us in great shape for getting one of the holiday bowl spots.

I glance over at my duffle bag. I packed in a hurry and probably forgot my underwear. I just grabbed some clothes, stuffed them in my bag, and got on the road prior to the game.

The sky is turning that soft shade of blue as the sun approaches the horizon. I yawn and adjust my ass in the seat of my truck, turning up the music on my radio to keep myself awake.

"Wake up, jackass," I mutter, giving myself a slap across my cheek. I see an exit sign in the distance, the one that leads to our farm. Only twenty more minutes to go and I'm home.

My phone rings and I glance at its holder clipped to my air vent. It's Mac. He must have just gotten up to do his morning chores. I hit accept.

"Damn, Mac-*inator*, you actually get your ass up on your own now?" I ask, trying to keep it light. I don't know how much Dad has shared with my brothers about his concerns over the business, and I don't want to alarm them. But I did text Mac to let him know I'd be home for a few days as a surprise visit.

"I just read your text. You're coming home for a few days?" he asks, an excitement evident in his tone.

"Just turning off the highway now, as a matter of fact."

"You should have warned Dad. He's planning to do inventory today. Killian, we have got to get a better system. I didn't want to tell you, but you'll see for yourself in a few minutes. Shit is bad here. And I know Dad is stressed. Fuck, bro, we all are."

Shit. My younger brother should be worried about who to take to homecoming and what colleges he's going to apply to this year, not about the farm or our father's stress level. Mac is a good kid, but as the middle son, I know the farm isn't where his dreams lie. He's wanted to be a veterinarian ever since he was old enough to know about professions.

"I'm working on some stuff to help him out, Mac. It'll be all right. I promise." I seem to say that word a lot to the people I love. Because my seventeen year-old brother deserves to be a worry-free teenager.

"Really? That's good news. I'll see you in a few." He pauses and I hear him shuffling around and heading down the creaking stairs of our farmhouse. "It smells like mom's making her famous banana pancakes with that homemade whipped cream. You picked a good day to visit."

I grin. God, I've missed her cooking, especially those banana pancakes.

"Save some for me. I'll be there in a few," I say and end the call.

The sky begins to grow lighter with each passing mile and I know the sun will rise not long after I arrive at the farm. I won't have time to sleep until after lunch so I grab one last energy drink and gulp it down as my mind wanders back to Grace.

I can't believe I said those things to her. What was I thinking? I groan. I'm such an idiot. I should have given her more time. I've probably lost any chance I had with her.

As I turn onto the farm and follow the long drive up toward the house, I wonder if Grace would ever even consider this life? She's all about tech and computers and city girl vibes. She clearly knows a lot about living on a cattle ranch, but that was her dad's dream, not hers.

Maybe this is all for the best in the end, I tell myself. I couldn't give her the life she wants no matter how much I'd want to. I'm just a farm boy from Iowa. Maybe that's basic, but it's me and I'm not going to change. I wouldn't want to.

If there's one thing I know, it's who I am and who I'll never be. And now that I have distance and clarity, I'm beginning to think maybe I'm not the man Grace needs, although I was so fucking sure I was.

I park the truck at the end of the dirt driveway, putting Grace in the back of my mind as my family all begins to spill out of the house to greet me.

"Killian!" Mom shouts as she runs down the front porch to embrace me. "What in the world are you doing here? What a great surprise!"

I return the hug, lifting her off her feet and making her laugh. My dad sidles up next to me, giving me a tip of the worn and dirty ball cap I gave him for Christmas one year and an appreciative nod.

My gaze goes to both of their faces and...shit. It really is as bad as it seems. I can see the lines of stress cutting over their foreheads and at the corners of their mouths. It affirms my decision to come home for this visit.

I set Mom down and give my special handshake to Jamie, who looks like he's just rolled out of bed. He grins up at me.

"You grew taller, sewer rat." I pretend to measure the new two inches of growth that now brings the top of his head up to my shoulders. Then I ruffle his bedhead hair.

He rolls his eyes, trying to flick my hand away from his head unsuccessfully. "Yeah, it's called puberty."

Mom scolds us both. "You two stop it and go grab some pancakes. I just finished making a batch."

His eyes brighten and, without another word, he runs inside. Mac stares at me and I pull him into a bro hug, thumping his back hard. He squeezes me and I know he's stressed too.

Clearly, Jamie is the only one who doesn't seem to know what's going on around him, which is fair. The kid's only in middle school. He doesn't need the weight of the world on his shoulders.

"Go on," Mom urges as she pats my arm and gives me a weary smile while she tucks some stray strands of hair behind her ear.

Dad pats my back as I walk up the steps of the old farmhouse that I've called home my entire life. It's not the biggest house. A few of the farms in the area have houses twice the size of ours. Mac and I have shared a room since Jamie was born. And my Dad added a shower to the downstairs bathroom when I was in middle school, so we at least have two showers now.

The exterior paint is starting to peel on the front porch from all the summer storms and winter weather, and the windows need some caulking. But as I step across the threshold and smell my mom's pancakes, my body relaxes and everything seems to make sense again.

Home. No matter how long I'm gone or how far from it I am, it always feels good to be back.

I head upstairs and pull some old clothes I've left behind out of my drawers, planning to jump in the shower and then get to work. But I take a minute to look around the room. Posters of video games still hang on the wall over my bed. The room seems smaller than it was before as I stand between Mac's bed and mine. He has clothes and papers strewn out on his bed and desk. His dresser is filled with colognes, deodorants, and underwear.

I chuckle. Some things never change, and something about that is very reassuring.

Knowing it'll be a full day, I take the fastest, coldest shower I can before grabbing a Thermos of coffee and eat a few bites of pancake before I head out to work. My brothers are already out by the barn taking care of their chores. I can hear a country song blaring from the stereo in the barn and Jamie sings along off-key.

"Can I get you to mend the fence down by the creek?" Dad asks as he motions toward the west field. "I noticed some rotten boards the last time I was out and just haven't gotten 'round to it."

I nod. "Yep. Sure thing."

"There's some wood planks in the barn," he adds. "Take my truck. I'll use the four-wheeler today."

I nod and head out to his truck, backing it up to the barn door, and I busy myself with loading wood into the truck bed, humming along to the music wafting out from the speakers in the barn.

"Need a hand?" Mac asks, picking up a few beams and sliding them into the truck bed.

Next thing I know, Jamie's jumping into the truck. "I call shotgun!"

I guess we're all going out to fix the fence.

"Get in back, ya runt!" Mac yells.

Jamie sticks his head out the window. "I called it first."

I sigh and shake my head, chuckling at my brothers bickering voices. "Enjoy the back, Mac-aroney." I pat the truck bed and Mac groans, but jumps up once we've secured the load.

"Don't try to throw me off this time," he grunts, giving me a pointed look as he dangles his feet off the back tailgate. The last time we did this, Mac went flying into the gravel ditch and ended up having to get ten stitches in his chin. Mom would totally yell at me if she knew I let him ride back there again.

"I'll do my best," I reply with a chuckle. "Can't promise anything, though."

"Asswipe."

"Turd bucket," I shoot back with a grin, enjoying the familiarity of our name games and the brotherly love between us. I climb into the truck cab, start the engine, and steer us across the field to the spot along the creek that needs mending.

Jamie, ever the chatterbox, starts peppering me with a slew of questions "So, how's school? Are you dating anyone? I heard you guys won yesterday. Did you play? How come Hendy or EJ didn't come with you?"

Hendy is Jamie's idol and he's said on more than one occasion that he wants to be just like him. As long as that's out on the field and he doesn't follow in his "playa" ways.

"Whoa, little dude. Chill. I just got home. Let me drink my coffee in silence before we play twenty questions," I

groan, rubbing at my temples to ward off the sleep depriva-
tion headache coming on.

"Sorry," he answers in a muttered slur, his feelings
clearly hurt. I park the truck, chug some coffee, and turn to
him, giving him my undivided attention.

"School is good. I like a girl, but we aren't dating. In
fact, I don't even know if she likes me back anymore. I did
play and we won, which was awesome because it could lead
to a bowl game in December. And Hendy and EJ had some
homework to do, so they couldn't come along." I fib a little
on that last one as I answer him back with the same rapid-
fire speed as he dished them out.

His mood lifts and he smiles. "So you like a girl?"

I laugh. "Really? That was the part you took away from
all that? You're a weirdo."

"Well, yeah," he replies as we get out of the truck and
start unloading the boards and working to repair the fence.

As we finish replacing the old rotted boards with new
ones, chatting about their school year and activities, the sun
begins to shine bright and warm across the field. It paints
the sky full of purple and orange, coloring the grass and the
barn in a natural light that I'd never be able to capture with
my phone. It makes me wonder if Grace would like it here.

I wonder what she would think of my family and my
brothers. And the farm.

I clench my jaw so tightly I could crack a molar. Why
am I thinking about Grace again? God, I wish I could just
drown my sorrows in my video game and have fun teasing
my online friend without a care in the world.

Dad's four-wheeler rolls down the dirt road, sending a
plume of dust behind it until it comes into view at the top of
the hill, parking next to mine.

"Looks good, boys," Dad says appreciatively as he inspects our work.

"Killian has a girlfriend," Jamie announces as he walks back to the truck.

I shove him from behind.

"Traitor."

Dad raises an eyebrow at me.

"Barf bucket," he lobs back, letting out an evil laugh and patting himself on the back as if he just did me a solid. "You're welcome!"

Mac snickers under his breath and I snap a glare at him too.

"What's this girl's name? Are we going to get to meet her?" Dad asks, helping us pick up the tools and remaining unused boards.

"It's...we aren't really dating. I don't think it's going to work out," I sputter as I try to think of anything to say that won't lead to more questions.

Dad claps my shoulder. "Sounds like we need to have a father-son chat about this one."

"No, Dad. We really don't. Let's go check that inventory since that's a hell of a lot more important to discuss than my non-existent love life."

He chuckles. "With an answer like that, I'm thinking there's more to discuss than you're willing to share."

The man is not wrong about that. Not wrong at all.

Chapter Twenty-One

Grace

I worked all night long on the software design, using the data I'd secretly confiscated from Killian's laptop to create a functioning program that I think will work.

Part of me feels guilty for using it without his permission, but I disregard those disruptive thoughts knowing it'll be worth any resentment he might feel if the program actually works. It's the only way I know to show him how much he means to me. How much I really do love him, even if I can't say it.

Which is the reason I called my dad earlier this morning under the guise of a regular check-in, knowing he'd be up at the butt crack of dawn. What I really wanted to talk with him about was Killian. Although my dad has always been my biggest supporter and sounding board, I've never spoken to him about matters of the heart. I never had the need to.

He answers in his typically chipper voice, background noises nearly drowning out his words.

"Hey there, Divine Grace! To what do I owe the pleasure of my daughter's call so early on a weekend?"

There's a pause and I hear the sound of a tractor motor turning off. He must be somewhere out in the pastures.

"Oh, shit. You haven't been arrested and need bail money, do you?"

I can't help but laugh at his antics. He's such a goof sometimes. Kind of like Killian. Both men have hearts of gold that can be overshadowed by their ridiculousness at times.

"Hardee-har-har. You're so funny. It may surprise you to know I haven't yet even gone to sleep tonight and it's not because I'm in jail trying to avoid being molested by other inmates."

He lets out a loud exhale. "Well, that's a relief. I'd hate to have to call your mother to tell her the news that her only daughter has turned into a hardened criminal."

Ahh, yes. My mother.

When I'm quiet and don't respond, he quickly jumps in "Is something going on, toots?"

He's impressively intuitive for a tech geek and always seems to suss the secrets right out of me.

"Dad, I don't think I know how to love someone."

Whoa. I didn't expect that to come shooting right out of my mouth in such a rush.

My dad, without missing a beat by my lack of finesse, smoothly transitions as easily as if I'd said the sky was blue.

"Honey, of course you do. You love me, your mom, Lucy, and Kelsie. You love animals and your grandparents. I think you secretly love the ranch, even if you won't admit it." I sniff at his overreaching assessment.

"So tell me why you think otherwise."

It's now that I get tongue-tied, unable to express how I feel about Killian.

"It's this guy..." I don't want to tell him who it is, though, because it might be a little much for a dad to know his daughter is in love with and also sleeping with her male roommate. "We've been seeing each other for a little while and I think it's serious...I've developed feelings, but I can't tell him that."

"So you're in love with him?"

I pause. An image of Killian lying next to me, brushing the hair out of my eyes and gently kissing me fills my head and my heart flutters like a million butterflies just took flight. "I don't want to love him. That's the problem. I don't know how. I can't give him what he wants."

"Is he pressuring you into something...physical?" He practically chokes out that word. "You don't have to do anything you're uncomfortable with, Grace..."

I cut him off. "No, it's nothing like that, Dad. He wants a relationship with me. I don't.'"

I hear a loud sigh expel from his chest—maybe out of relief or something else.

"I see..." he says in a soft whisper. "Why is that?"

Tears prick at the back of my eyelids. I swipe away one that threatens to fall down my cheek, confused why suddenly I'm overly emotional.

When I don't immediately answer, he knows exactly what I'm thinking. God, how does he do that?

"Honey, is it because of how your mom's and my marriage ended? Because if it is, I need you to know something," he says adamantly, his fatherly concern etched in his tone. "You are not us. You are someone entirely different. Our mistakes are not yours. The relationship issues your mom and I had were nothing to do with you. You're the only good byproduct of that union."

"Byproduct? Ewww...what am I? Processed meat?"

My dad laughs at my attempted good humor. "Sorry, poor figure of speech. But my point, Graceland, is that you are not me or your mother. All relationships are unique and different. Just because ours didn't work out doesn't mean yours won't. Just look at Nana and Papa Ford. They were married fifty-five years and lasted a lifetime."

His voice tightens because I know what he means. Papa died three years ago and Nana followed closely behind two months later. It was both romantic and so very sad for our family.

He continues, "Love is the best gift in the world to both give and receive, but you have to be open to it, Gracie. Don't prevent yourself from experiencing it fully if you've found it in someone."

It's like a light bulb flicks on in my brain, illuminating the dark fears I've carried around with me for so long. The worry that I'm not perfect enough or worthy of being loved. Because, sadly, that's how my mom has always made me feel. She only loved me if I met her overly high and unattainable expectations and there were always strings attached. If my dad couldn't make her happy in their marriage, how was I supposed to do it as her daughter?

My heart leaps into my throat and my voice quivers as if the vocal cords are being plucked like violin strings "But, Dad, what if..."

"Grace, you can't do that or you'll drive yourself crazy. What ifs are like invisible ropes that tie us up and keep us from accepting love when it's offered. They will drag you down if you let them. You have to free yourself of those ties and go into it with arms wide open."

After ending the call with my dad, my heart feels full and my spirits are lifted. I add the final details to the program and run several tests to make sure it works. This is my gift to Killian and his family. If I can offer even a small token of my appreciation by increasing their farming productivity with my inventory and purchasing software, then this will all be worth it.

I'm too keyed up to go to sleep and Killian and the guys aren't expected to return home from their out-of-town game until around ten this morning. I'd heard they won the game via texts from Lucy, who road-tripped with a few of the other players' girlfriends to watch in Eastmount. It was last night after the game when she and EJ went out on their special anniversary date and then partied at the hotel.

My lungs feel as if I'm sucking in ice each time I breathe in the frigid air. Early November can get hella cold out here in this mountainous region. The school is in a valley nestled between two mountain ranges, which means we are normally dry this time of year. While we might not have any snow yet, it still gets mighty windy with the gusts coming off the tops of the mountains.

I keep my eyes focused on the track in front of me. I decide to run the campus track so I can be here when the football team arrives on their buses. Based on the time on my watch, they should be here in another fifteen minutes so I kick it up a notch and keep running.

I'm completely depleted of energy when I see the buses rolling down the long drive to the football stadium parking area where the players get dropped off.

I make my way toward the drop-off point where fans and families are hovering around, all animatedly chatting about the team's win. I wait on the outskirts of the crowd, hoping to appear nonchalant so I don't look overeager to see

Killian when he gets off the bus, even though my heart is beating a thousand miles an hour.

The two long, white coaches with the CFU school logo on the side come to a screeching stop in the circle drive, the doors swinging wide with a metallic-sounding hitch. Guys begin piling off one by one, all looking a little tired but pumped from their win, their legions of fans greeting them in their excitement.

I notice Hendy climb off the coach closest to me and a girl runs up to him, looping her arms around his neck. He smiles when he sees me over the girl's shoulder, winking in my direction.

"What the hell are you doing here, Gracie?" he asks curiously, disconnecting the girl from his body and closing the distance between us.

I shrug and hook my thumb behind me toward the track. "I came out for a run and noticed you guys coming back. Thought I'd get a ride back with Killer."

Hendy narrows his eyebrows. "You'll be waiting a while then because he didn't ride with us on the bus. He dropped off Nathan somewhere after the game and drove home."

I'm thoroughly confused because I was home all morning and Killian wasn't there.

"What do you mean? Like *home* home? Not school?"

Hendy chuckles. "Yeah. Like the farm in Iowa. Said it was something important he had to do."

I stare off over Joel's shoulder toward the mountain range. The girl next to him bounces at his side, grabbing onto his hand as if claiming him for herself, waiting for his attention to be drawn back to her. We both ignore her.

Finally I reply, feeling oddly sad that Killian didn't tell me. But then again, why would he? I basically told him just two days earlier that I didn't love him and didn't want to be his girlfriend. I have no right to know what's going on in his life.

Shit. I've ruined everything. This sucks.

"Oh, okay, cool. I didn't know that." I cast my gaze down at the ground to keep myself from tearing up. When I glance back up at Hendy, the girl is whispering something in his ear that has him grinning with lifted brows. "I'll see you later, Hendy."

"Yeah, see ya at home, Gracie," he says, giving me a quick wave and then returning his attention to the girl. She must be a new one because I haven't seen her around before. I shake my head, unable to keep up with his long stream of conquests.

I start a light jog back to the house and mentally calculate how far of a drive it might be to his farm.

I have nothing else going on today or tomorrow. The only class I have on my schedule is one I can miss without an issue.

Decision made, I get home and quickly pack a few things in my overnight bag and stuff my laptop in my backpack.

If the mountain won't come to Mohamed, then Mohamed will go to the mountain.

The drive wasn't too bad except for the last hour of the trip. Once I got into western Iowa, and all I saw for miles and miles was a flat line of wheat and corn fields, it was tough to stay awake. It made me seriously appreciate my dad's ranch and its sprawling green spaces and sloping hills that lead into the base of the mountains.

I look down at my phone and check the route one more

time. Hendy had sent me the address and directions before I left, promising he wouldn't inform Killian I was on my way. From the map, it looks like the turn onto the Palmer's property should be coming up on the right about a half mile down the road.

It's getting near dinnertime, so I'm hoping they are all home and won't mind me just showing up unexpectedly. I pull off to the side of the road for a quick assessment of my appearance in the mirror. I'd showered before I left and weaved my damp hair into a long braid, so now as I remove the twist tie holding it back, the thick strands unravel as the dark waves flow past my shoulders. I add some shiny red lip gloss and smile at my reflection.

There are two ways my unannounced arrival will go: Killian will either be happy to see me or pissed that I came. Either way, he'll be surprised as hell.

Now I'm second-guessing whether I should have called before driving all this way. Maybe it was a stupid ass idea and I should turn right back around and go home, leaving Killian none the wiser.

But just as the thought leaves my head, I hear a horn blare, startling me out of my reverie.

I turn my head to look out my passenger window. A wood fence outlines the property and just on the other side of it sits a red pickup truck, three pairs of eyes all staring at me. One of those pairs belongs to Killian, who looks dazed and thoroughly confused at my presence as if I'm a ghost or apparition.

He shoves his head out the open window, turning his ball cap around on his head so it's on backwards as I roll my window down so he can see me.

"Grace?"

I give him a timid wave. "Hey, farm boy. Surprise!" The

inflection at the end of my greeting is more question than statement. His eyes narrow like I'm a math problem to solve.

"What the hell are you doing here?"

Before I can answer, he turns to look at his brother sitting next to him in the cab of the truck to respond to something he asked. Probably wondering who I am.

The other brother gawks at me from the back of the sturdy truck. He is the spitting image of Killian, except slightly smaller and younger, his hair a little more unruly and far more ginger than my roommate's.

My car idles as I try to come up with the words to explain why I'm parked on the side of the road near his farm, nearly eight hours away from our school.

"Well...you didn't come back home after the Eastmount game and I needed to show you something."

Yeah, that explains everything.

He gives a dry laugh. "And you couldn't have waited until I got back to school?"

I shake my head. "No. It's kind of a present."

The brother inside the truck lets out a long, "*Ooooooooh*...a present! She must like you."

Killian elbows him in the side and the kid doubles over with a loud, "Umph."

And then, without asking, the boy in the truck bed jumps out and leaps over the fence, opening my car door while saying to his brother, "I'll show her up to the house. Mom is gonna shit her pants!"

With that, he slams the car door and grins over at me broadly.

"Hi. I'm Mac. You must be the girl Killian likes."

Oh, wow. Things are going to get interesting.

Chapter Twenty-Two

K illian

I stare in shock as Mac escorts Grace up the steps to the front porch.

"You gonna let Mac steal your woman!" Jamie teases. I glare at him.

"I'm pretty sure that won't be an issue," I assure him, leaving the part about her not wanting anything from anyone in the relationship department unsaid as I start after Mac and Grace with Jamie in tow. Dad pulls the quad up beside my truck as we reach the porch.

"Who the heck is that?" he shouts over the loud motor, motioning to Grace's very fancy Volvo.

"A friend from school," I reply.

"His girlfriend," Jamie adds, drawing out the "girl" part. Dickwad.

I grab him around the neck, tucking him inside my armpit, and mess up his hair with my knuckles.

"Hey!" he screeches and then sucker punches me in the gut and runs inside.

"I'm gonna get you!" I yell as I hear Dad chuckling behind me.

"Don't be too hard on him. He misses you. We all do." Dad motions toward the kitchen where I can hear Mac, Jamie, Grace, and Mom talking.

"So, is this *the* girl?" he asks quietly, taking the porch steps toward the door.

I nod and think better of it, adding a shrug.

"Well, let's go meet her."

He claps a weathered hand on my shoulder. I take a deep breath and follow him inside where I find Grace sitting at the kitchen table while Mom piles baking dishes in front of her, including fresh baked bread and what smells like her famous chicken and wild rice hot dish.

"You must be starving after that drive," Mom says, a wide smile on her face. When I walk in, she glances up at me and mouths over Grace's head *she's so pretty*.

I can't really dispute that. Grace is the prettiest girl I know. I nod and hang my jacket and hat up on the post in the entryway then make my way into the warm and delicious-smelling kitchen.

"Smells good, Mom!" Jamie exclaims, reaching over the table to pick out some cherry tomatoes from the salad bowl and popping one in his mouth like a pig with no manners.

Mom laughs, shooing him away with a spatula. "Thanks. But you know the drill. Go wash those grimy hands before Grace thinks we're all animals. I still have to slice the bread."

"Yes, ma'am." Jamie complies and rushes down the hall to the bathroom.

Grace watches him leave and giggles, her gaze locking with mine as I take a seat next to her. I watch her survey the room, taking in her surroundings, and I wonder if she's comparing it to her Dad's place. I know he must be wealthy and I'm sure they live in a fancy home.

I try to take in my childhood home through her eyes. The worn cream-colored paint on the old farmhouse cupboards. The one-hundred year-old pine floors that creak when we walk in front of the refrigerator. It may be outdated in some respects, but it feels loved. From the well-worn pans to the dishes that were my grandmother's, this place is filled with family history.

Regardless of Grace's opinion on the matter, I realize I'm not embarrassed by it. I'm proud of our home. I'm really proud of what my family has achieved. There's simply the matter of figuring out a way to help us through this rough patch. This farm is not only our family's livelihood, but our family legacy, inheritance, and the future I want to continue. It's who we are and I can't imagine living my life any other way than farming.

"Hey," I whisper softly near her ear, sitting back upright to study her profile. She turns and gives me a shy smile.

What the hell is she up to? I'm about to ask when my mom produces a basket of sliced sourdough bread.

"Here you go, dear. There's butter right there in the dish by the salad. And pick whatever salad dressing you like," she says, gesturing toward the array of condiments in the middle of the table.

"We even have honey from our beehive if you want some on the bread," Jamie announces as he returns from the bathroom, reaching for a piece of bread and slathering it with butter and honey. "Mom just collected it yesterday."

"Oh, wow. It's so cool to have your own homegrown honey. Thanks," Grace replies. She reaches for the bread and follows Jamie's lead. My mom holds up a pitcher of iced tea.

"Would you like some tea, Grace?"

Grace nods. "Yes, please. Thank you so much, Mrs. Palmer. Thanks for inviting me to dinner. I'm so sorry I just showed up uninvited."

"Oh, don't be silly. It's nice to have a guest. We seldom get anyone out here who isn't family, a neighbor, or someone we do business with," Mom offers with a giant smile, her eyes glittering with that knowing look only moms get when their son brings home a potential partner. "Or in this case, one of Killian's college friends we haven't met yet."

Dad joins us at the table wearing a clean shirt and his face freshly scrubbed. Shit, I suppose I should've cleaned up a little better, but I was so shocked by her appearance that I was on autopilot.

"Welcome to our home, Grace," my dad says, smiling over at us both. "Any friend of Killian's is a friend of ours. So, what brings you all the way out here? We're not exactly just around the corner from CFU."

My thoughts exactly. I'm glad my Dad asks the obvious question that I haven't gotten around to. Dad takes a giant scoop of casserole and plops it on his plate.

To say I'm shocked and confused about Grace sitting at my kitchen table in Bumfuck, Iowa, is an understatement. I didn't even know she knew where I lived. Although we've talked about where I grew up, I know I've never given her my address.

It's a mystery.

Grace wipes a hand on a napkin in her lap and then offers it out to Dad. "Yes, nice to meet you, Mr. Palmer."

I feel like an idiot. I should've done the formal introductions to my family, but I'm still too befuddled to put words together.

When Grace turns back to me, her eyes search mine as if she's trying to offer me an explanation telepathically, but I can't figure out what she's thinking.

"Well, while Killian was away at his football game, I began working on something back at school and I was so excited to show him. But then when he didn't return to school after the game...well, it seems a little silly now, but I... well, I wasn't sure when he'd return and I couldn't wait...so here I am." Her words come out in a rush, stammering a little before she stuffs a bite of bread in her mouth, chewing purposefully as we digest this bit of news.

I eye her suspiciously because I still have no idea what she's referring to. What was she working on? But before I have a chance to dig further, my entire family begins the Spanish Inquisition, peppering Grace with rapid-fire questions, starting with my mom.

"Grace, where are you from?"

Without hesitation, Grace begins telling them about her childhood in San Francisco, moving out to country life and her dad's cattle ranch, and the small town where she went to high school. My dad asks about her major, and they *ooh* and *ahh* over her geniusness. And then Mac teases her about how she survives living with me in my messy room. I raise an eyebrow at him.

"Excuse me, bro? But I'm not the messy one," I snarl and curl my lip up menacingly.

"What?" he exclaims with a laugh and then makes an oinking sound. "You are! You're a pig."

"Takes one to know one," I reply, because he brings out my juvenile behavior. My parents ignore this and from the sounds of their own laughter, I can tell they are both happy I'm home and they already seem to like Grace as if she's been a part of the family for years.

It makes me sad that it won't last long.

Finally, as things settle down and the conversation lulls while everyone continues to eat and go in for second helpings, my dad brings it back around to the work he still needs done on the farm while I'm here.

"Would you have some time this evening to look at the tractor? Maybe give Grace a tour around the farm," Dad suggests hopefully.

"Sure. I can do that. Grace can get the grand tour," I say, shoveling the last bite of food into my mouth. I wash it down with the full glass of iced tea and push back from the table, grabbing my plate. I check Grace's progress and see her plate is empty too. "Are you all done?"

She nods and I add her plate to my handful and drop them in the sink.

"Who's on dishes tonight?" I ask my brothers, knowing Mom has a rotating chore schedule for kitchen duty. I glance over my shoulder at the two boys who are still happily stuffing their faces.

"It's my day," Mac grumbles in between a mouthful.

"I wish I had siblings to share dish duty with," Grace says. "It was always just me and my dad."

I notice the empathetic look exchanged between my parents. It was clear when she was discussing her childhood that her parents weren't together and thankfully neither mom or dad pry any further. It's a sore subject with Grace, even though she hides it well. Especially her relationship with her mom, which is strained, to put it mildly.

Jamie purses his lips and considers Grace's comment. "Wow, I never thought about that before. I guess we are kind of lucky there are three of us."

Everyone bursts out laughing at how grudgingly Jamie admits this. I look around and smile. Grace has slid right into our family like a puzzle piece no one knew was missing. Something about that makes the hole in my heart seem bigger. There must be an important reason she's here, but I don't think it's about her missing me. She made it clear she doesn't want me as a boyfriend and doesn't want a relationship.

Regardless of how perfect she seems to fit here, I'm resigned to the fact that this is all just temporary with Grace. No matter how much I feel toward her, anything more meaningful won't ever happen.

"Come on. Let's get out of the madhouse and you can fill me in on what's so important," I say, ushering her out the back door toward the barn. The sun is setting, moving lower into the horizon. Crickets chirp and a handful of fireflies hover around us in the bushes near the grove of trees. We're quiet as we begin to walk, listening to the sounds of cattle lowing and chickens squawking in the background, the cool fall evening air blanketing us. Our farm dog, Quincy, bounds ahead of us in search of bunnies or cats to chase as we make the short walk to the big red barn behind the house.

I want to reach for her hand and hold it in mine. To nuzzle my nose at the hollow of her throat. To press her up against the bales of hay and let my fingers go wild over her soft flesh.

But I don't do any of that and roll the barn door open instead. Rubbing the back of my head, I examine Dad's old tractor, wondering what's been going on with it and knowing he doesn't have the money to replace or even fix it right now if it's broken. Being that I'm mechanically inclined and pretty quick to determine the problem, I poke around the engine of the old piece of farm machinery that was purchased around the same time I was born.

Before I can even assess it, Grace sidles up next to me on my right. "You think something got loosened? Maybe a bolt? Or a loose cable?" She scratches her head and looks around. I watch as she finds a tool box and brings it back over. "I'll start checking for any loose connections. I feel like that's always the culprit when my dad's tractor breaks down."

I stare at her in a total awe like she's an angel sent from above as I'm hit with an urge to wrap her in my arms and never let her go.

This woman is perfect. God, why the hell did you deliver the perfect woman and then deny me the satisfaction of making her mine? What a mess.

I groan.

She glances up at me. "What?"

"Nothing," I mutter, clearing my throat. "I'll check some of these cables."

Fifteen minutes later, the tractor roars to life, a puff of smoke busting from the engine exhaust. Grace claps her hands in celebratory glee and spins around to give me a high five.

"See? I told you. Just needed to tighten some things up and *bam!*" she says with a squeal of delight.

Fuck, why does she have to be so cute?

"I'm impressed. Thanks for the help." I wipe my hands on my pants and look down at her face. I still don't know why she's here. What did she come for and what does she have to show me?

My voice turns serious and low. "Grace...I know you didn't drive all this way to help me fix a tractor. Why *are* you here?"

She adjusts her weight from one foot to another and looks up at me nervously. "Killian, I'm not good at expressing myself with words like you are. I mean, you know how to chat with people. You talk to everyone everywhere. It's just your natural personality."

I shrug. "I mean...I guess."

"Words are like...your love language...and actions...well, they are mine," she manages before she bites her lower lip. I'm really not sure where she is going with all this love language stuff. I'm still so fucking confused.

"Okaaaay..."

"Well, that's why I'm here. I created something I need to show you." She jumps down off the tractor and brushes her hands on her leggings. "Do you have a computer or laptop here?"

I give her a pointed look. "Yeah, of course we have a freaking computer here. This is a farm, not a medieval village," I snap, but then pause, realizing I sounded harsher than I meant. I think the events of the day have gotten to me. "Sorry, yes. We have laptops, a gaming computer I built, and my dad's business computer. My desktop computer is a beast, but it works."

"Cool. Then can I show you what I've done?" She chews on her lip again.

Why does she seem so nervous? And did she just admit she likes me with all this talk about love languages and shit? Am I reading too much into this, or did she create something as an action to show me how she feels about me?

I hold out my hand. "That's why you're here, right?

Come on, let's go back inside so you can show me your love language."

I guide us out of the barn, across the yard, and back inside the house. Everyone has gone off to their normal evening activities. Mom and Dad are watching the news, Mac is finishing up in the kitchen, and the sound of Jamie's video game travels through the thin walls when we reach the top of the steps.

When we step inside the bedroom I share with Mac, she lets out a long gasp and then covers her hand over her mouth, trying to stifle her laughter as she surveys the room. "I see the messy genes are strong in this family."

My own gaze scans the room and lands on Mac's side, pointing toward his mess. "Hey, that's his mess, not mine. Look, I even made my bed. Sorta."

Grace snorts when she glances at my half-made bed. "You're getting better, I'll give you that."

When her gaze lands on my computer system I spent an entire summer building, she points at the system appreciatively. "Wow, that *is* a beast. I'm impressed."

"Why, thank you," I say, pulling back my desk chair for her to take a seat. I pat the top of one of the monitors. "I saved all my chore and paper route money my freshman year of high school and even attended a computer show and bought all the parts. I spent hours watching YouTube videos and it took me a month to put it together. But it works."

Grace claps me on the back as she scoots by me and takes a seat, adjusting the chair at the desk. Then she begins to type as I watch in wonder over the top of her head as she goes to town. Her dark hair is pulled back into a sleek ponytail, her sweet scent permeating my bedroom.

There's no doubt I'll have trouble sleeping tonight with

her scent still lingering in my room and thoughts of her running rampant in my head.

I watch with fascination as she types furiously on the keyboard, entering some domain in the browser as a file pops up on the screen.

When she turns her head, I stare at her beautiful profile. I've missed her face.

"This is what I wanted to show you and tell you about. I created it. For your dad. For your farm."

She grows quiet and introspective while I try to comprehend what I'm looking at. The screen is filled with data and a slew of numbers. As I finally piece the words together with the information on the screen, I realize I'm staring at... an inventory app.

"Wait...what..." My words trail off as my mind races and I run a hand through my hair, allowing myself a moment to put this all together. "How did you..."

I'm completely dumbfounded and in awe, but have so many questions left unanswered.

How did she get all this information? How did she know we needed to fix our inventory problems? Hell, how did she know the problem even existed?

"Please don't be mad at me, okay?" she begins quietly, her forehead wrinkling apologetically. I stare blankly at the screen, running through various scenarios in my head as to why she would have done this.

"The other night...when we were in that fight, you left your computer on. I sort of saw some stuff...not on purpose...but it was there and, well, I wanted to help. So I extracted the data and I developed this software program. It should help your dad with his issue."

My eyes follow where she points on the screen with her finger. "I ordered the printer for the barcode scanner. It will print out a barcode sticker from here when you click on it. It will number everything in sequence and then it...here, I'll show you," she adds as she begins to demonstrate the capacity of the program.

She's literally taken all the research I've been working on this semester, used the data my dad sent, and turned it into a functional and operational system.

I'm not sure if I should be pissed as hell at how fucking smart she is or terrified by her level of genius.

Whatever the case, it just might fucking work. I can't even be mad about her snooping into my school computer when I see how impressive this report is.

"It will work," she says and I realize I said my last thought out loud. "I tested it."

"I just...this is fucking incredible, Grace." My gaze bounces between her face and the computer screen.

"I told you, my love language is action. And in this case, the action was to create software for your dad's inventory situation."

Clasping my hands on the back of the chair, I spin her around so she is looking up at me, her dark eyes gleaming with something I can't quite make out. I cup her face in my hands.

"Grace." It's barely a whisper.

"Yes?"

"I'm going to kiss you now," I declare, brooking no argument.

"Okay," she replies anyway, and I press my lips to hers.

We should have heard fireworks or felt the earth move by how powerful it is. Instead, we hear Mac making a gagging noise before shouting from the doorway.

"Oh, God! Ew! Mom! Killian is kissing Grace in *our* room!"

Grace starts giggling against my lips and I stand back up to my full height, rolling my eyes at the ridiculous behavior of my younger brother.

"Welcome to the insanity that is my family."

"I think I like the insanity," she responds, her eyes searching mine. "But you...you, Killian Palmer, I'm going to love."

I quirk my eyebrow, not wanting to get my hopes up, but still dying to know what this means.

"What happened to roommates with benefits and no relationship?" I ask, needing to clear things up so I know exactly where I stand, even though my heart seems to beat louder with each word. My hope blooms like flowers in the spring.

"Well, I might have fallen for my roommate...and after careful consideration, I've decided I want more than just benefits. I want a *killer* boyfriend," she teases.

"I think that can be arranged."

I pick her up in my arms and hold her in my embrace as I kiss her once again, hungry and insatiable, ignoring the loud protests and demands for me to stop coming from Mac, who's still standing in the hallway like an eavesdropper.

Nothing and no one will ever make me stop loving this girl.

Chapter Twenty-Three

G^{race}

After spending a few hours demonstrating the capabilities of the inventory program and software I designed to Mr. Palmer, I earned a grateful hug of appreciation from Killian's mother and a very hearty handshake from his father. Then Killian and I spent the rest of that evening down in the basement, reacquainting ourselves with each other.

AKA *messing around.*

Killian sternly advised his brothers to stay the fuck out of the basement or else they'd get decapitated by the hay baler at the hands of their older brother. His threat sounded very gruesome and like medieval torture to me, but it did the trick and they remained upstairs the entire night, allowing us privacy for some fun makeup sex.

As I lay in his arms on the couch, an old movie from the

90s playing on TV, our bodies warm and sated, I casually run my fingers over the coarse copper hair on his chest, my head nestled into the crook of his arm.

"Hey, I notice you have *Capital Offense*," I remark innocently, pointing toward the stacks of games on the floor by the television. "Want to play?"

Killian pushes up on his palm and stares down at me. "You play CO?"

"Duh. Who doesn't?" I tease with a lift of my shoulder before sitting upright and swinging my legs to the side of the couch.

Killian follows and then jumps off the couch, grabbing the controllers and flipping the switch to project the game on the screen in front of us. He spins around with a big grin and tosses one of the controllers at me, plopping back down beside me and logging in with his username.

BigHardware69.

I stifle my grin, knowing full well already what alias he uses in the game after finding him still logged in the other night. He puts it in two-person mode where we can play directly against each other instead of on teams.

It's so weird that of all the gamers who play this, the one I ended up connecting with online is my very own roommate.

And now, apparently, my boyfriend.

He nudges me on the arm. "You gonna login so I can kick your ass, soda pop?"

I snort, giving him a side-eye. "Yeah, right. You have no idea who you're up against, *farm boy*."

"Oooh...I'm so scared." He trembles in mock terror. "Like I'm gonna let a girl beat me."

"Well, you have before," I murmur with quiet confidence, entering my login credentials as his eyes stay focused on me, pinning me with disbelief.

"How's that? I've never played this game against you. I didn't even know you were a gamer."

I feign innocence. "I beat you last week. You just didn't know it was me."

Killian now looks thoroughly confused. "Huh?"

I point to the login screen on the television, where it blinks with my alias name of **RanchHandRAM1**. The avatar is a generic one with no identifying characteristics that would lead him to believe it's me or even a female player.

"I have a confession to make," I say, turning to face him. I chew on my lip, watching as his face morphs from confusion into understanding. "I'm RanchHandRAM1."

"No fucking way!" he exclaims, his whole body brimming with energy and disbelief. Like he was just zapped with an electric current. "How is that possible? I thought I was playing against a dude this whole time!"

Then his eyes turn dark as they roam appreciatively up my body before landing on my boobs. He licks his lips. "You just got a hundred times sexier, soda pop."

I bark out a laugh as he tugs the controller out of my hands and tosses it on the floor before he presses his body into mine. He kisses me deeply, tongue swirling inside my mouth, as I thread my fingers through his wavy hair.

When he breaks the kiss, I smile up at him. "I thought you wanted to play the game?"

He undoes his pants where I see the outline of his very hard bulge. Killian reaches for my hand and places it over his erection. I graze my fingertip over the protruding head, already feeling the wetness from his arousal. He bucks into my palm and I squeeze him in my fist as he groans loudly.

"Yeah, we'll play. But first I want to show you just exactly why my alias is BigHardware69."

* * *

A week later, I'm sitting downstairs in our house back at school, laptop open on the kitchen table when I get a message pop up. Although I'm doing homework, I'm logged into my game.

> BigHardware69: Hey, RanchHand. Is your amazing football playing boyfriend home?

I chuckle, looking around the empty kitchen. No one else is here right now, which is precisely why I'm downstairs and not in my bedroom. It's very rare to have quiet alone time in this house.

> RanchHandRAM1: Nope. He was at football practice the last time I checked. Why? What did you have in mind while he's gone?

Killian must be logged in from his phone on his way home from practice. I grin as I read his incoming message.

> BigHardware69: I've got ideas…like you being naked and ready in your bed before he gets home.

The naughty suggestion has my panties getting damp, my nipples hardening at the image he's planted in my head.

I look at the time on the kitchen clock and see I have an hour before we need to leave to meet my dad and his new girlfriend, Melissa, for dinner at a restaurant in town. He'd called me the day after we returned from my visit to Iowa and mentioned he wanted to introduce me to her.

At first I was shocked when he said he'd been seeing her for a while on the down low, not wanting to upset me or something. But after the heart-to-heart conversation we had, knowing I'd found someone I loved, he said it helped him to realize that he too had found someone special.

I quickly type out my response.

> RanchHandRAM1: Okay…but hurry. This gamer is in need of some BigHardware to fill her RAM up.

Giggling to myself, I close my laptop and race upstairs. Throwing off my clothes, I grab for the jersey hanging over my chair, slipping it over my naked body before jumping into my bed. Then I hear the front door open and slam shut. Loud, thumping boot steps come clomping up the stairs and the door of our bedroom swings open.

Killian stands in the doorway as we take each other in. He's freshly showered after an afternoon practice, his auburn hair darkened and damp, swept back on his head. He's wearing a CFU red T-shirt and track pants that provide ample room for his thick thighs and hard cock, both outlined perfectly against the nylon material. He toes off his boots and I crook my finger at him. He stalks toward me.

"I thought I told you to be naked," he says sternly, quirking a brow as he whips off his shirt, tossing it on his side of the room.

I seductively lift the hem of his jersey and spread my legs to prove I listened to his directions.

"I am…but I wanted to wear the jersey of my favorite football player." I grin and then let out a yelp when he grabs my ankle and slides me down to the end of the bed. He tugs the material up over my breasts and latches onto a stiff nipple. He sucks it with fervor as I arch my back off the mattress and fling my arms and legs around his body, wanting to get him closer still.

"Do you know how much I love seeing you wear my number?" he asks, moving to the other nipple. I run my hand down his solid backside, grabbing onto his ass and tilting my hips to meet him.

"As much as you love seeing me *not* wearing it?"

I roll my hips to meet his erection and he huffs out a laugh that turns into a groan.

"Good point."

He moves in a flash and neither one of us has any clothes on any longer.

We both let out loud moans of satisfaction when he slides into me and, for a moment, we're both still, relishing the connection and the feel of each other's bodies.

It doesn't take long for us to reach the precipice together, his fingers deftly bringing me to climax as he thrusts several times before releasing inside my wet warmth.

"Fuck, Grace," he murmurs, his lips pressed against my ear as our breaths begin to even out once more. "I love you so much."

Tears of happiness suddenly fill my eyes and threaten to escape. I smile and kiss his shoulder, breathing in his delicious scent.

"I love you too, Killian."

As we snuggle in each other's arms, enjoying the afterglow of sex, I think about how scared I'd been to trust someone with my heart. Afraid to give it and not have it returned.

Had you asked me at the beginning of the school year if

I might fall for my football-playing roommate, I would have laughed at the absurdity of the notion.

But Killian knocked through all my defenses. He proved to me that he was the man I needed all along and although he is a brute on the football field, he's a big teddy bear with a huge heart.

That's my guy—#69. BigHardware69. Farm boy.

And I'm forever his RanchHand.

Epilogue

G race - December

The holidays are in a week and although I'm excited for Christmas break and going home to visit my dad, it will be the first time in months that Killian and I will be apart for more than a few days.

I'm already missing my Big Hardware right now and he's only been away for the past two days. He and the rest of the CFU football team are on the road for a bowl game being played in Washington State.

While Lucy and I would love to have traveled to see them play in the game, we stayed behind to finish our finals and host a small watch party at the house for some of our friends.

"Hey, do you have the chip dip out there already?" Lucy calls from the kitchen where she's been busy all morning baking Christmas cookies. The entire house smells of peppermint and sugar, and I'm sure I'll gain the entire "freshman fifteen" back within a day.

I bend over and pick up a chip, digging it through the creamy cheese dip before plopping it into my mouth. I yell back with a mouthful, "Yep. It's out here and it's delish!"

I'm about to head back into the kitchen to grab some plates when my phone rings. It's the sound of an incoming video chat.

My heart starts to race when I think it might be Killian calling me back so I can wish him luck. But when I look down at the caller ID, it's actually Kelsie.

I answer it with a click, her face coming into view, blonde hair swept back in a sleek ponytail.

"*Bonjour, mademoiselle! Joyeux Noel!*" Kelsie greets me with a perfect Parisian accent, a wide smile on her red painted lips.

She looks happy and beautiful as always.

"Merry Christmas yourself, girlie." I turn my face to the side and call out to Lucy. "Hey, get in here, Luce. Kelsie's on the phone!"

I plunk down on the sofa and take in the woman in front of me. One of my best friends and the girl who went off to learn about life, art, and culture in the City of Lights.

Lucy bounds into the living room, wiping her hands clean on a paper towel before springing onto the cushion next to me. She grabs the phone out of my hands.

"Merry Christmas, Kels! We miss your stupid, pretty face."

Kelsie rolls her eyes. "Whatevs. You two are shacking up and getting the regular D, you wouldn't have had time for me anyway."

Lucy and I glance at each other and begin to laugh. I lift a shoulder. "Yeah, you might be right."

"Speaking of the D's, where are your boys right now? I can't believe both of my smart besties bagged dumb football players. I'm so embarrassed to know you two." Her tone is sarcastic to match the playful roll of her eyes.

Lucy scoffs. "I'll have you know they are both very intelligent men and you're making broad assumptions about the boys we love."

Kelsie makes retching noises in mock protest. "Uh-huh. They'll have to prove it to me when I return."

The last we heard, Kelsie would be coming back to school at the beginning of next semester and we all needed to figure out another living situation. Since the house was full until next year, she'd have to either go back to the dorms or share an apartment with some other girls. It wasn't something we were excited about because we wanted her to live with us but there wasn't any other option at the moment.

"What will you be doing for Christmas?" I ask, staring over at the oversized fake Christmas tree in the corner of the living room. The one we all haphazardly decorated because none of us could commit to one type of decor. It looks like an odd art project that a little kid created.

Kelsie's face turns up into a beguiling smile and her eyes gleam with excitement.

"Well, I've met someone and he's going to spend Christmas with me and Auntie D."

Lucy and I couldn't be more shocked if she'd said she was an alien from Mars. Our eyes snap to each other, mouths falling open and we turn back to look at her.

"Back the truck up there, missy," I scold, because this is the first we've heard about this guy. "You met a French guy? Someone you're willingly introducing to your family?"

Her eyes close and she sighs dreamily. "Yeah. I did. He's not French, though, and I think I'm in love."

I guess there's a first for everything. This is certainly big news because it's not the same woman who left us when she went to Paris.

That Kelsie once said she would never fall in love because she was too much of a free spirit, independent thinker, and a woman longing for adventure to ever want to settle down.

Lucy gasps and then quickly snaps her mouth closed before asking the logical question. "Who is he?"

"His name is Hayes. He's from the States too. We met this summer in a street cafe and hooked up a few times which, as you both know, is my style. But then he showed up in my International Business classes and things went from there. Crazy, right?"

I nod. "Sounds like fate. I can't believe you didn't tell us sooner."

Kelsie waves a hand dismissively, but then she looks away, her eyes downcast.

"Honestly, I didn't expect to fall for him. Now that I'm getting closer to moving back home, I think it's going to be hard to leave him. We've spent nearly six months together. He's amazing. So smart, super hot, speaks fluent French like nobody's business. And holy hell, that man can make me come with his..."

Lucy makes a nervous screeching noise to interrupt. "TMI, Kels!" She shakes her head and blocks her ears with her palms. Kelsie cackles with delight.

"Oh, Luce. Still our sweet, innocent girl, aren't ya?"

"Hardly," I scoff. "You should hear her and EJ go at it! They sound like porn stars and I hear *everything* because I'm right above them!"

Lucy shoves against me with her shoulder and I groan. Kelsie laughs on the other end of the line.

"Need I remind you that you and Killer are right above us? You guys are louder than a whole football field of players."

After a few minutes of laughter, the conversation gets back to the topic at hand. Kelsie's return to the U.S. and what she plans to do with her newfound love.

"What do you think you'll do?" Lucy asks quietly, obviously concerned for Kelsie's welfare.

She shrugs. "I guess we'll just have to figure it out as we go. He's from Colorado so it's not too far. If we wanted to keep seeing each other, we could."

"Or..." I suggest. "Maybe he could transfer to CFU. Obviously we have a great international business program here."

Kelsie shakes her head. "I doubt it. He is very close to his family and I know he misses them a lot. Although he didn't come right out and say it, I could tell this semester abroad was really hard on him. He was kind of broody at times."

Hoping to change the vibe, I go back to the holiday conversation.

"Well, I'm sure you'll have an amazing Christmas in Paris. Bring us lots of *pain au chocolat* when you come home, okay?"

There's a knock on the front door and it reminds us of our company.

"Hey, Kels, we gotta go. We're hosting a watch party for the bowl game today."

Before heading to the front door, Lucy kisses her hand and flings it at the camera with a loud smack. "Love you, girl. Merry Christmas! Have a great time with Hayes."

"Love you too."

I give Kelsie a long look, knowing how much it hurts when you're far away from the ones you love.

"It'll all work out, Kels. And we'll be here for you when you come home. Love you and Merry Christmas!"

"Love you too. *Au revoir.* See you guys soon."

The End

Want to read Kelsie and Hayes's story?
Add ***Falling for the Football Player*** to your TBR now.

More CFU Crew

But wait...there's more!

The entire group of friends now have their own stories to read, including Kelsie and Hendy. Check out the entire CFU series now.

Falling for the Fake Boyfriend (Book #1)
Falling for the Roommate (Grace & Killian)
Falling for the Football Player (Kelsie & Hayes)
Falling for the Quarterback (Hendy and Lottie)

About the Authors

USA Today & International Bestselling romance author, **S.E. Rose** lives near Washington D.C. with her family.

When she's not wrangling her cats or keeping up with her kids, she's plotting her next story.

She loves all things wine, coffee, and cats.

In her non-existent free time, she enjoys traveling, going to concerts, binging on her favorite shows, and reading, especially if it's a good mystery or comedy.

Learn more about upcoming books from S.E. Rose at www.seroseauthor.com or follow her on Facebook and Instagram.

Sierra Hill is a ***RONE Award-Winning*** author of ***Game Changer***, as well as over 40 novels, including the college sports series, ***Courting Love***, and her newest hockey series, ***Vancouver Vikings***.

Subscribe to her email list and download a FREE book here: https://www.sierrahillbooks.com//newsletter

www.ingramcontent.com/pod-product-compliance
Lightning Source LLC
Chambersburg PA
CBHW030138010826
48973CB00002B/626